Praise for
RECLAIMING EROS

Candice is the kind of woman who walks her talk. Reclaiming Eros is more than a collection of stories. It is a deep dive into the heart of our erotic power, which is often shamefully relegated to the shadow parts of our psyche. It is clear that Candice has courageously plumbed her own depths and presents here a road map for any who wish to blaze a similar path.

~ Catherine Oxenberg, Actress, Author, Philanthropist/Activist, & Producer of *Sexology*

Candice uses a mix of poetry, short fiction, and sociological analysis to uncover some of the most powerful feminine archetypes alive within us. Non-linear but brimming with intellectual and emotional clarity, her poems and stories trace an intuitive path for the reader to follow down past her social conditioning to wilder, more authentic versions of herself. Enjoy the ride.

~ Robin Rinaldi, Author of *The Wild Oats Project*

Not for thousands of years has the end of patriarchy been so clearly in sight. But we are still suffering from the millennia of its distortions upon our sexuality—shaming, hiding, repression, judgment. Candice's unflinching look at the ways our eros has been pushed into the shadows—and her vision for what eros could be when brought into wholeness again—is as timely as it is necessary.

~ Michael Ellsberg, author of *The Education of Millionaires* and *The Power of Eye Contact*, co-author of *The Last Safe Investment*

The thing about writing about archetypes—which Candice does very well—is that they reach off the page, grab us by the short hairs, and remind us that they live in our blood and always have. This book is smart. Your brain will approve. This book is hot. Your body will place this book in your lap and lap it up. This book is empowering. Your womanhood will head off to bring more balance to this planet and heal the divide between the folks on it.

~ LiYana Silver, Coach, Torch-holder, & Author of *Feminine Genius: The Provocative Path to Waking Up and Turning On the Wisdom of Being a Woman*

reclaiming
EROS

Copyright © 2018 Candice Dawn
All rights reserved.
ISBN: 1985730928
ISBN 13: 978-1985730922

Cover image by Rae Diamond
Cover & interior design by Darrin Drda
Author photo by Wendy K. Yalom

reclaiming EROS

[**A Heroine's Journey**]

by
CANDICE DAWN

For Her

I take pleasure in my transformations. I look quiet and consistent, but few know how many women there are in me. ~ Anaïs Nin

*Look: the constant marigold
Springs again from hidden roots.
Baffled gardener, you behold
New beginnings and new shoots
Spring again from hidden roots.
Pull or stab or cut or burn,
They will ever yet return.*

*~From the poem, "Marigolds,"
by Robert Graves*

table of contents

Acknowledgements xiii
Introduction xix

PART ONE: INVOCATION

Prologue: Woman 1
Reclaiming the Feminine Power of Eros 7
Erotic Deprivation and the Commodification of Sex 15
The Miseducation of Sex: Abstinence,
Pornography, and Romance 23
Discovering Eros Through Archetypes 37
Erotic Initiation 41

PART TWO: INITIATION

The Virgin Archetype 47
   SLUT 52
   Lilith 54
The Whore Archetype 71
   In the Garden 77
   Magdalena 78
The Warrior Archetype 111
   Legend of the South Seas 117
   Diana 119

The Queen Archetype 139
   Fairy Tales 143
   Rani 145
The Nun Archetype 177
   On a Sultry Southern Sunday 182
   Christina 184
The Mother Archetype 211
   Great Mother 219
   Nnenne 221

PART THREE: INVITATION

The Morning After 247
Epilogue 251

acknowledgements

First, my heartfelt gratitude to you holding this book right now. To take a chance on this subject and to graciously offer your time reading these words—it is a gift I do not take for granted. Thank you.

To my three editors: Jordan, I could relax into my creativity and wrestle with these wild ideas knowing that your keen eye and attention to detail would help me sculpt them. Adam, I am grateful for your passion and commitment to this subject as well as for your willingness to work with me in the final stretch to ensure that my message was both accurate and accessible to readers—and I will definitely do better about those ellipses… ;-) And Gravity, wow, we really birthed something here, didn't we? Thank you for believing in me, offering me your unvarnished opinion, and guiding me through the frightening process of editing a collection of fiction. I bow to you, mama.

To Darrin: Thank you for creating your visual magic on the book interior and cover designs while patiently taking my vague feedback. It's a joy to finally work with you after having admired your work all these years.

To Rae: Thank you for the gorgeous marigold cover image. I'm amazed at how you took one idea and ran with it—sketch after sketch after sketch. It's an honor to display your work on the cover.

To Lisa Marie: Thank you for your astute and honest feedback. Your work was pivotal in helping me take Nnenne's story to a whole new literary level. Deeply grateful.

To Robin, Liyana, Michael, and Catherine: Thank you for taking time out of your busy schedules to read early copies of this manuscript and for offering your kind words of encouragement and endorsement.

To Sequoia and Wendy: Our photography sessions uplifted the project and inspired the creation of these characters. Thank you for your creative collaboration and for helping me embody these archetypes in real life.

To Ashley Joy, Hayley, Jessica, and Melissa: Your gorgeous hair, makeup, and wardrobe design during the photo shoots guided me to access the range of emotion I needed to call in these archetypes. These stories would not be the same without you.

To Jennifer: Though we didn't end up working together, your guidance during the consideration process provided valuable feedback and helped me further refine my message. I am grateful to you and your publishing company.

To Jeff Brown and Lori Ann Lothian: Your creative guidance early in this project gave me the courage to continue writing—one word in front of the other.

To my lovers: Whether you know it or not, our memories lie between these sheets. Thank you, each of you, for being my teachers.

To the numerous folks who so generously donated to my crowdfunding campaigns—thank you for believing in this project long before the vision became fully clear: Adam Gordon, Jamie Holdorf, Tom & Yvonne Hogan, Steve, Lisa & Stephen Jr. Holdorf, Lloyd & Rochelle Gordon, Ben & Jennifer Rode, Ben Hart, Ilya Yacobson, Gabrielle Faith Cohen, Cory Michelle Johnson, Rain Phutureprimitive, Philippe Lewis & Paget Norton, Kate Russell, Mai Vu, Cind, John Peterson, Shoshanna French, Camille Macres, Alex Sousa, Sarah Hall, Johanna Lyman, Terre Busse, Caitlin Powell, Jim Soviero, August Schulenburg & Heather Cohn, Lauren Searles, Randy Scott Ralston, Jason Nunes, Guy Jara, Annie Willis, Cassandra Steer, Beth Altshuler, Angela Renae Amarillas, Lauren Wilson & David Mizne, Destin Gerek, Cheryl Good, Justine Cooper, Anthony S. Walker, Kate Mackay, Elizabeth Ames, Andrew Kerr, Vince Martin, Sallee Spearman, Theres Kull, Grace Weintraub, Meghan Scibona, Lauren Sheehan, Stuart Rusty, Jennifer Sheridan, Curtrice Renae Goddard, Traci Redmond, Deborah Windham, Vidura Barrios, Leah Thompson, Holli Christine McCormick (Metamorphic Coaching: www.hollichristinemccormick.com), Devi Ward, Rebecca Farrar, John Hagel, Marinella di Matteo & Ilya Druzhnikov, Alana Logan, Ashley Apple, London Elise, Susan Seybert, Bruce Meyer, Shirley Miller, Wes & Amy Hart, Alisha Gordon, Alan Brewer, Andrew Crowley, Kanna Scoville, Debra Giusti, Brandy Lueders, Jessica Garfield-Kabbara, Ken Glickfeld, Samantha Nalo, Britt Zakai, Yingkuan Liu, Duncan Krieger, Holly Rudinoff, Avi Santana, Andre Rego, Michelle Berry, Perry Gordon, Kim Merkin, Christina Mihu, Lhotse Hawk, Siobhan

Curley, Sarah Jones, Dana Muscatello, David Brestel, Bill Lamond, Tanith Flynn, Christina Shipp, Marc & Naomi Lewis, Deanna Ogle, Elina Tserlin, Verena K. Adina Rivers, Philipp Solay, Lauren Lee Anderson, Thea Gramley, Abby Kojola, Gaby & Raj Sundra, Lisa Formers, Ryan Christopher, Jane Taylor, Nicole Walker, David & Lani Yadegar, John Taylor, Kim Iglinsky, Mia Roman, Marta Szudek, Arielle Palmer, Emily Green & Jean-François Gaultier, Danielle Keen, Ali Shanti, C. Picara Vassallo, Gigi Abdel-Samed, Sonya Stewart, Danica Winters, Luke Anderson, Amjad Obeidat, Mia Cara, Marc Bejarano, Eric Elliot, Sarah Greene, Ryan Harris, Forrest Ratliff II, Jenny Ferry, Luis Andrei Cobo, Anne O'Farrell, Auren Kaplan, Sean X Cummings, Tara Divina, Bertram Meyer, Joseph Harris, Jakob Wowza, Sarah Young, Adithya Raghunathan; and to all the anonymous donors and donors who made contributions under $20.

To everyone whom I met during my time at OneTaste: The lessons I learned about desire, turn-on, and orgasm guided me many times during my life and throughout the writing of this book. I am grateful that you all were a part of my erotic journey.

To the women in my life: How I have continued to be awed and inspired by your fierceness, your passion, and your commitment to bringing the feminine out of the shadows and into the forefront of our lives. A huge thanks especially to my women's group, Tara, Mia & Alia. What an honor to have watched each other grow these past several years.

To my grandmama, Vonnie: Thank you for teaching me how to love whole-heartedly, how to forgive, and how to place faith in something greater than myself. I am a more compassionate woman because of your guidance. Thank you for never giving up on me.

To my mother: Thank you for teaching me what it means to be a strong woman who demands respect. Thank you for teaching me that my voice—and every woman's voice—matters. Thank you for supporting my dreams every step of the way. I am a more courageous woman because of your guidance. Thank you for never giving up me.

And finally, to the men in my life.

To my father: Thank you for the gentle, loving support throughout the years. The number of times I've heard you say, "I'm proud of you," is too many to count. I know I can always count on you to love me no matter what.

To Om: Thank you for teaching me how to access my power through surrender. You are a wise, potent force—and friend—in my life.

To Jon: Thank you for sticking with me during some of the most difficult years of my life. I know it was not easy. I am truly grateful for your commitment and loyalty. I wouldn't be here without you.

To Gabriel: Thank you for walking with me during the final, crucial year of this project. Your support and faith in my work as an artist continue to inspire me. I admire you and can't wait to see what we create together. No matter where this journey takes us, I am grateful to be sharing this moment with you now. I love you.

And finally to Adam: You supported me through most of this project. You bolstered my spirits when I saw my publishing dreams dashed. You provided a home for us so I could focus solely on my writing. You held my hand so many times when I wanted to give up. I am profoundly grateful for the role you played in my life and for the deep love that we shared. I look forward to supporting each other's dreams in this next phase of our relationship. I love you.

introduction

My heroine's journey began more than fourteen years ago. Yet as a twenty-three-year-old newlywed, hiding from her sexuality behind the guise of a relationship and simultaneously starving herself to avoid facing her own erotic power, I did not know that at the time. I had decided that I wanted to be an actress, but since my new husband and I couldn't afford to continue living in New York City, we moved to Florida. I was miserable—and if I had to bet money on it, so was he.

I remember the moment clearly: I was sitting in a hair salon surrounded by women who seemed to have it all—money, security, and the freedom to go anywhere they wanted anytime they wanted. And yet, these women, nearly three times my age, spent their days obsessed with maintaining their appearance equivalent to a thirty-year-old.

Internally, I laughed. "How sad," I mocked. In fact, I deemed my youthful self superior to them as I judged their futile attempts at happiness. The sticky veneer of complacency and privilege coated my mouth. As I involuntarily tried to wash it away with a sip of my complimentary wine—freshly dispensed from a box—I caught a glimpse of my foiled head and gaunt face in the mirror.

Despite nearly turning away, my eyes remained fixated in horrific fascination. It was like staring at a ten-car pileup trying to determine if the bodies on the road had any life left in them.

"When did I become a walking mid-life crisis?" I thought to myself. "Who was I becoming? Or worse yet—who had I already become?"

I pictured myself forty years in the future sitting in that same upholstered high-chair, wearing those same ridiculous foils, and holding that same glass of cheap wine. Only my roots were grayer, my face more plastic, and my mind more intoxicated in order to withstand the pain of a life unlived.

While I had laughed at them, I realized I did this only because my greatest fear was that I was just like them.

I hated myself. I wanted to die. Instead, I wrote.

When I returned home, I immediately penned the poem, "A Woman That Was," which was initially included in one of the stories in this book. That story, "Christina," is based on the Nun archetype and "A Woman That Was" was Christina's catalyst for erotic awakening. During the editing process, I replaced that poem with the more literarily appropriate, "OUT." But the sentiment behind "A Woman That Was"—and its power as a catalyst in my own life—is still very much a part of the essence of what you will read in this book.

After writing that poem, it would be only a few months more until my husband and I moved back to New York City. But it would take several years before I would find the courage to face my appetite. After being amenorrheic for three years, ending my relationship with my husband, and sleeping on friends' couches for six weeks with everything I owned stored in the basement of a Brooklyn church, I figured that the universe was sending me a pretty strong signal to seriously examine the direction of my life.

I was twenty-eight years old. Saturn had indeed returned and he declared twenty-eight my "Year of Fear." His first assignment for me was to make a detailed list of everything of which I was afraid. Then, I chose to do everything on that list. I did it to challenge the suffocating defenses I had built around me. I did it because I knew my desire lay precisely behind that veil of terror. And I did it so that I would not become A Woman That *Was* but A Woman That *Is*—alive, vital, and present in every moment.

Most of the poetry in this book came from that Year of Fear—a truly transformative period of my life. I'd begun the journey to erotic maturity and my sexuality was—and continues to be—a potent gateway to womanhood. Ultimately, I discovered that sexual liberation had less to do with becoming liberated so that I could enjoy sex and more with learning how to sit in the uncomfortable center of my own sexuality so that it could liberate me.

And thus was born *Reclaiming Eros: A Heroine's Journey*. While these stories are fictional, they are based on my own experiences of erotic awakening. I chose to distance my personal self from the women within these pages in order to reveal a much broader sense of the word "woman."

Mainstream society has a painfully limited view of the potency of femininity—usually attributed to thin, white, heterosexual, cisgender, able-bodied women between the ages of 18 and 35. I recognize that I, as only *one* woman—who also happens to be mid-30's, white, cisgender, able-bodied, and bisexual—cannot possibly encapsulate all that is "woman" in one slim volume. But my hope is that by sharing a glimpse of what is possible, it will clear the path for other women to rise and share their stories.

Caroline Myss, a medical intuitive whose healing modality is largely based on Jung's work, describes archetypes as "dynamic living forms of energy that are shared in many people's thoughts and emotions, across cultures and countries…these patterns, often ancient in origin, populate our minds and lives in ways that affect us deeply."[1] The feminine archetypes in this book—Virgin, Whore, Warrior, Queen, Nun, Mother—guide us on this mission because they reflect qualities innate to *all* of us. When the reader sees a piece of herself within each of these characters, she may decide to take the first steps on her own journey to erotic awakening.

These archetypes had much to teach me during the writing process. Some of the stories came quite easily—Virgin, Warrior—while others were a struggle—Queen, Nun, Mother, Whore. These archetypes demanded that if I were going to speak using their voices, then I had to get in alignment with them in my own life.

The Queen showed me where I was still holding on to Princess-like entitlement and petulance. The Mother helped me move through my own fears of becoming pregnant and facing death. The Whore guided me to heal the anger I have often felt around masculine sexuality. And the most personal story, the Nun, taught me about compassion and self-accep-

---

[1] Myss, Caroline. *Sacred Contracts*. New York: Three Rivers Press, 2002. 6. Print.

tance, as reflected by those beautiful women at the hair salon and my years battling anorexia.

The working title of this book was *From 6 to 9 and Beyond: Widening the Lens of Feminine Eroticism*. For me, it was an homage to our modern relationship with the erotic and an invitation to tread beyond our comfort zone. The first thing many notice when they read the title is that the numbers "6" and "9" feature prominently and remind them of the sexual position known as "69," where two people perform mutual oral sex. To reference the term "69" is to invoke countless jokes. My deliberate choice in using "69" was to acknowledge the "tee hee hee" high school mentality many of us have regarding sex and to say in agreement, "Yes! Sex is kind of funny sometimes."

If I'm honest, I don't see anything inherently wrong with our current relationship to sex, as long as it is safe, sane, and consensual. I am not here to shame or denigrate *anyone's* sexual tastes, preferences, or explorations, nor do I claim to have the decisive answer on what authentic sexuality means. What I will say, though, is that I believe mainstream modern society has a very *limited* scope of what is possible in the realms of the erotic and the sexual—especially when it comes to feminine desire. This book endeavors to include current perspectives while also widening the lens to reveal new possibilities.

On a technical note, the former title also refers to the book's "6" stories and "9" poems guiding us on the journey through these archetypes' erotic awakenings. Indeed, a great many more archetypes exist than just the six I name. However, these were the ones that I felt represented a range of women and provided a solid base of feminine expression. Mixing attributes of the Queen and Nun creates the Priestess, while blending the Whore and the Warrior reveals the Femme Fatale. Virgin-Mothers are archetypal hybrids common to many religions and cultures. It would take a thousand lifetimes to understand the great mystery that is *Woman*; these stories are compelling expressions within the richness of *Her*.

So think of this book as both my prayer and offering to all who read. It is not the definitive guide to anything, really. It is simply a slice of my own journey and an invitation for you to begin yours. I encourage you to sit with these archetypes, discover how they might show up in your life, and listen to what they may have to teach you.

Finally, make no mistake about it: living an erotic life is a courageous act. Presence, surrender, sitting in the unknown—most do not learn to value these qualities. They are not what ensure survival in an action and goal-oriented society. To cast off the cloak of security for the naked rawness of vulnerability is an act of rebellion and a cultural taboo. Although the bravery required to embody our own eroticism is no small feat, the rewards are more powerful than we can possibly imagine.

Welcome. And thank you for your bravery.

PART ONE

invocation

> *For women, the best aphrodisiacs are words. The G-spot is in the ears. He who looks for it below there is wasting his time.* ~ Isabel Allende

woman

I looked into the mirror today,
Focused on the mystery
Waiting patiently behind the ocular aperture;

Quieted the voices that told me
I should have a smaller waist
And a smoother face.

I asked the question,
"Who is Woman?"
And awaited the ineffable reply.

She first came to me as a dragon's eye.
"Beware the lower depths,"
She counseled.

I flashed a bravado smile
And asked again,
"Who is Woman?"

Then came the hummingbird,
Flapping her wings
At my arrogant back,

And cautioned,
"Those who ask this question
Must be willing to die."

Steeling my jaw,
I did not heed her warning,
But demanded once more,

"Who.
Is.
Woman."

A silent scream ripped through my ears
As her thick-bitter tea joined
My lips in holy prayer.

A face, too beautiful to bear,
Delicate features contrasting my own,
Slashed my vision.

Crumbling to my knees, I cried,
"No! Please! Spare my life!
I will give you anything."

Hoisting me to my feet, She growled,
"Wake up, Girl. Do not bow to me.
Remember: True Service is not Sycophancy."

The black blood, pooling between my thighs,
Now rose above my chest,
Flooding my frozen throat.

She whispered, "Your hard heart
Is still learning to let the love in.
Drown the Child and your freedom begins.

The boys, they are calling,
Aching to suckle
Your milky breasts.

And when they are grown, they will call,
Aching for you to suckle
Their milky heads.

You can not blame them.
You can only love them.
As I love you.

Surrender.
Surrender.
It is the easiest thing in the world.

It.
Is.
Woman."

The balm of healing seared,
Icy-hot, through my heart,
And panicked blindness gave way to simple sight.

The Virgin appeared before me,
Her innocent gaze teaching me how
To see with fresh eyes.

Next, the Whore,
Celebrating her body,
A vessel for divine inspiration.

Then the Warrior,
Bloody blade at her side,
Dripping with uncompromising truth.

Followed by the Queen,
Glittering in gold,
Power unapologetically adorning her throne.

Afterwards, the Nun,
Prostrated, her twisted fingers
Spelling out her memoir of devotion.

Finally, *Abuelita* herself,
Wise and wizened,
Birthing and destroying all of creation.

As the riddle unfolded and the veil lifted,
My choked voice gave way to breath
As I inhaled Her final words:

"Only trust the bearers of light
Who have also fallen in love
With the dark."

Salty-sweet tears of recognition
Slid down my mottled cheeks,
Cleansing my bitter soul,

Until I was met,
Once more,
With my own solemn reflection.

I looked into the mirror today,
Focused on the mystery
Waiting patiently behind the ocular aperture;

Quieted the voices that told me
I should have a smaller waist
And a smoother face.

I asked the question,
"Who am I?"
And what I saw was simple:

I am Woman and She is Me.
You are Woman and She is You.
We are Woman and She is We.

reclaiming the feminine power of eros

> *The feminine is the most formidable of the forces of matter. True enough.*
> *"Very well, then," say the moralists, "we must keep out of its way."*
> *"Not at all," I reply, "we must master it."*
> ~ Pierre Teilhard de Chardin[2]

What is erotic?

Is it sex? Or an electrifying conversation?

Dancing the tango? Or a silk scarf wrapped around your wrists?

Doing the work you love? Or just a damn fine piece of chocolate?

What if it's all these things—plus driving to work? Having an argument? Grieving a loved one? Washing lettuce?

What if it were *every moment of your life?*

This is the power of eros.

Eros—the root word of erotic—is a Greek word meaning a kind of love connected to our fundamental creative impulse. It is what enlivens and animates the cosmos.

---

[2] de Chardin, Pierre Teilhard. "The Evolution of Chastity." *Toward the Future.* Trans. René Hague. London: Harcourt, Inc., 1973. 74. Print.

Surprised? That's normal. Most of us associate the word "erotic" with something having to do with sex. Erotic photos or films are typically more culturally palatable versions of porn. Erotic novels are usually romance stories with graphic sexual content. And erotic stores run the gamut of culturally-acceptable sex toy shops to seedier XXX video stores.

But relegating eros to the realm of the sexual limits its power. Of course there is nothing sinful about sex and eros can certainly thrive within sexuality. But when we divorce eros from our everyday lives and view the erotic as acceptable only behind closed doors, we have relegated our vitally creative energy to a tiny pocket of our lives—a pocket often fraught with confusion and shame.

We are creatures of habit and often how we do one thing is how we do everything. More specifically, how we interface with sex—an energetically-heightened arena—can model how we interface with many other aspects of our lives.

If we tend to hide behind a mask of "knowing it all" in sex, most likely we tend to "know it all" in a range of other situations. If we do not know how to ask for what we want sexually, most likely we don't know how to ask for what we (truly) want in other arenas of life.

But if eros permeates every aspect of our lives, why is the erotic usually only found in terms of sex? The answer is twofold.

First, in its liberated state, sexuality serves as an analogy and gateway to eros; the link between the two is quite easy to make. Imagine the best sex you've ever had. Or at least the kind of sex you *want* to have. It might include some of these qualities:

- Unwavering presence and focus
- Lost in the moment with no sense of time
- Connection to something bigger than one's self
- Surrendering to unhindered flow
- Intimacy, vulnerability, and the shedding of masks
- Every move is the "right" move without having to "think" about it
- Psychological, emotional, physical, and spiritual growth
- Breaking of old boundaries and newfound feelings of "possibility"
- The willingness to take one's time
- Innocence and novelty
- Inspiration and/or revelation
- Connection to love
- Being possessed, as if taken over by "genius"[3]
- Freely expressing desire
- Trust
- Lack of judgment
- Lack of goal or agenda
- Playfulness and taking part in the experience simply for the pleasure of it
- Merging with the moment and a sense of "oneness"
- An infinite and abundant feeling

---

[3] Author Elizabeth Gilbert references the ancient Roman definition of "genius" as a guardian spirit that can be invoked and possess one with creative power. Gilbert, Elizabeth. "Your Elusive Creative Genius." Lecture. *TED*. Feb. 2009. Web. 1 June 2016.

Even though the list above is meant to reference sex, we could just as easily be describing other peak moments in our lives. When we ask ourselves, "What makes me come alive?" we aren't interested in measuring quantifiable means of success but in experiencing the feeling within a quiet surrender. This is the healing gift inherent to reclaiming and restoring eros to our everyday lives. We awaken in ecstatic aliveness and rend the veils between self and other. We can celebrate our differences and honor our boundaries while recognizing all of life as one pulsing, gorgeous consciousness.

So how did we go from sex modeling eros to sex being the only place one can find eros? This question brings us to the second reason why the erotic is usually found only in terms of the sexual. **In its shadow state, sex serves as an unfulfilling substitute for eros.**

An increasing number of people around the word live in cultures that prioritize *logos*, or rule-based observable knowledge, over *mythos*, or emotion-based intuitive knowledge. As societies optimize profit and production—*logos*-based measurements of success—they marginalize the *mythos*-based values of connection, intimacy, and mystery. In fact, many people in positions of power and privilege view the *mythos*-based qualities of empathy, compassion, and relationship as liabilities.

There is no doubt that the rise of *logos* was an important part of humanity's evolution; in particular, it has helped to reframe literal translations of creation stories as gorgeous allegories of the human condition. Most people no longer think the gods are going to smite them every time there's an eclipse.

Logos is useful for following maps and balancing budgets. Logical thinking has driven modern medicine to improve vaccines, antibiotics, and other technological marvels. And most people now accept a heliocentric view of the solar system.

But the cultural influence of *logos* is no longer in balance. Rather than being a counterpart to *mythos*, *logos* has dominated cultural values at the expense of mystery and mystical experience. While the mythic mystery of creation can yield ecstatic experiences, it can also bring us face to face with our dark subconscious—a wide, terrifying unknown replete with unyielding tests of faith. As a result, the unfathomable mysteries of life have been relegated to sex as various forces stifle, control, and manipulate that single arena.

While many have suffered from this banishment of eros into sex, it is the mythic world of the *feminine* that has experienced the worst of it. Writer and queer activist, Audre Lorde, once wrote, "When I speak of the erotic, then, I speak of it as an assertion of the lifeforce of women; of that creative energy empowered the knowledge and use of which we are now reclaiming in our language, our history, our dancing, our loving, our work, our lives."[4] Lorde's call for the reclamation of the feminine erotic life force beyond sex is a timely one.

It has become apparent that now, more than ever, people are feeling called to participate in a sacred duty: to lift

---

[4] Lorde, Audre. "The Uses of the Erotic." Metahistory.org. Web. 1 June 2016. [Original Source: Lorde, Audre. *Sister Outsider: Essays and Speeches*. Berkeley: Crossing Press, 1984. 53. Print.]

mankind from self-destruction by harnessing the erotic wisdom of our ancient mothers, sisters, and daughters and remember what it means to be women—formidable forces of creation.

This call is not only for those who have a vulva or who identify as "woman" or "female." To speak of the "feminine" is to refer to energies inherent in *all* people. The same can be said of "masculine," as well as "androgynous" and the various iterations and expressions that lie within and beyond that range. Every human has the capacity for surrender and creation in some form. Eros' power extends its invitation to those who listen closely to the gaps between words and knowledge. So please don't feel excluded by the limitations of language.

Wounded patriarchy—founded on prioritizing *logos* and demonizing *mythos*—threatens our species' survival and evolution. Immature tyrants—who are often emotionally suffering due to their own disconnection from eros—abuse their excessive power in service of a bottom line that numbs their pain and loneliness. The ravages of climate change, racism, and misogyny are all connected to the banishment of eros—for how can humanity possibly live in harmony with itself and the planet when it has lost the ability to empathize? Now is the time to bring the feminine into the forefront of our lives, not because she is superior, but because she has been relegated to the shadows for far too long. When the feminine is in harmony in everyone, regardless of gender, balance is restored and people no longer need to outsource unmet "feminine" needs—

often entangled in limiting stereotypes—to other people, such as wives, girlfriends, mistresses, and mothers. Balancing the internal capacity to express masculine, feminine, and androgynous needs opens doors to personal responsibility, spiritual maturation, and cultural evolution.

erotic deprivation and the commodification of sex

Even though mainstream binary-based culture seems to identify gender as "masculine" or its polar opposite, "feminine," what culture is actually saying is that one side is "masculine" and the other is "not masculine." This binary places the masculine in a position of power (and oppression) by othering anyone who identifies as feminine and erasing those who fail to fit within the masculine mold, which makes for a strange dance when people look to meet "gender-specific" needs. Many people don't dare to lower themselves below the "masculine," *logos*-driven world of quantifiable success. To admit that they hunger for "feminine," *mythos*-driven qualities such as connection, empathy, compassion, and relationship is to strip themselves of a privileged position—forcing them to reckon with their place within the realm of "the other." The failure to do this can lead to a state of erotic deprivation.

Shadow capitalist society—"shadow" meaning unacknowledged and unintegrated—has devised a fantastic means for momentarily quelling the pain of erotic deprivation: commodification. If an otherized, non-masculine need that yearns for fulfillment can be bought, then *logos* retains its position of power by framing "feminine" needs as subordinate in its own hierarchy because money equals success, success equals power, and power consequently reinforces the dominant masculine system. And since eros is often erroneously equated with sex, the commodification of sex—the culturally ingrained purchasing, bartering, or stealing of sex to fulfill erotic needs—becomes *de rigueur*.

The pattern typically goes like this: erotic deprivation leads to feeling depressed, inadequate, scarce, lifeless, or generally unlovable in some way. People are taught to equate this erotic emptiness to some sort of problem that can be fixed only in the sexual realm. This places a high value on sexual interactions that will temporarily satiate the hunger and reinforce a false sense of power.

With the commodification of sex, sexuality becomes a bargaining chip for a whole host of needs unrelated to sexuality. In essence, sex becomes a pawn in power games such as:

- Assuaging loneliness
- Boosting self-esteem
- Attempting to validate ethical righteousness
- Demonstrating success
- Buying partnership
- Punishing through withholding
- Feeling:
  » safe
  » powerful
  » alive
  » worthy
  » important
  » loved
  » morally superior

RECLAIMING EROS

When a person is seen as only being or possessing an erotic commodity, she is objectified and the entirety of her soul is converted into a product that can be acquired. She becomes a means to an end, rather than a reflection of her own expression. The unifying quality of eros is immediately exterminated in the separation-preserving, *logos*-based system of commerce. The rationalization of this logic often goes, "I am one person and you are another. I have this commodity and you have that commodity. If I give mine to you, I expect you to give me yours. Or if you offer yours, I cannot receive it without giving up mine." While this system of belief might be fine when buying a car, if tit-for-tat rules our sexual and erotic experiences, failure is inevitable because (a) commodification reinforces separation leading to the death of eros, and (b) sexuality can never hold the entire universe contained within eros.

The heteronormative realm, which is (unfortunately) the standard model of relating, includes men buying expensive dinners and gifts—or being "nice guys"—with the expectation that they will get sex further down the line if they "pay" enough. This fosters the belief that men are entitled to sex and is an integral contributing aspect to "rape culture."[5]

On the flip side, women might have sex even when they don't want to so they don't "hurt the guy's feelings" or lose out on finding "the one." Conversely, women might withhold sex

---

[5] Rape culture is a sociological concept that refers to a society where rape is normalized based on misogynistic and culturally-acceptable notions of femininity and gender. Aspects of rape culture include victim-blaming, slut-shaming, and teaching women how to "prevent rape" rather than holding men accountable for their own unacceptable actions.

in order to keep their "virtue" and snag husbands (as the saying goes, why buy the cow when he can get the milk for free?).

Many people swing in the other direction and go ultra-spiritual with their erotic desires—in effect, people can deny that these desires even exist. Ever hear the old spiritual-bypass phrase, "It's all an illusion"? Similarly, many might claim that they are "above the body" and have mastered their baser sexual impulses. Whatever the method of choice, people have been taught to mitigate erotic needs by placing them in the sexual realm and using sex—or the absence of it—as the currency for meeting those needs.

To be clear: the commodification of sex is *not* paying money for sex or sexual acts. This is known as "sex work," a legitimate business that also happens to be subject to the commidfication of eros—just like any other profession. In fact, sex workers who voluntarily choose their profession often come to have clear boundaries between the erotic and the sexual. Simply put, sex workers can see sex from a different and special perspective as just sex. And while sex itself may be a gateway to the erotic, they know it is not a *substitute* for the erotic.

Because of their perspective and experience, sex workers can potentially use their gifts for deeper erotic healing. For thousands of years, sexuality was a tool for transformation and awakening. Tantrikas, dakas, dakinis, and temple priestesses would sometimes have sexual contact with seekers—initiating them into mystical realms of knowledge. In modern times, sex surrogates are employed to help heal the psychological trauma that is often locked in their patients' bodies. While adult performers can invite people to explore fantasies, prostitutes, dominatrices, and other sex workers create safe spaces for clients to be witnessed in their desires, fears, and shame.

However, like anything that is pushed into the shadows, the stigma that comes with paying for sexual services or being a sexually empowered woman keeps sex workers laboring in the black market of society. Many are trafficked into sex work against their will or choose sex work as a "desperate last resort" to make ends meet. And those who possess the gift to heal through sexuality and enter the field willingly must do so at the risk of facing jail time or having fundamental civil rights revoked, such as using online payment processors, getting a loan, or opening a bank account.[6]

Bringing consciousness to our relationship with sex and shining a light on these shadows is a solid first step towards learning to infuse sex with eros. When beginning the journey, this fundamental question can be helpful:

Am I using my sexuality as a means to become more present and self-aware based on my desire, or am I reacting out of craving and using sexuality as a means to numb and escape reality?

Simply asking this question can immediately shift habitual commodification to newfound presence. But this does not mean it's all screaming orgasms and making love like a tantric master. In fact, choosing presence and feeling the magnitude

---

[6] Morris, Chris. "Porn and Banks: Drawing a Line on Loans" CNBC. 17 May 2013. Web. 1 June 2016.

of collective erotic deprivation takes courage because it often entails breaking down the protective façade that stands in the way of true erotic power. The void of wanting brings people *tête-à-tête* with the sadness, emptiness, and loneliness that can arise when pride and vanity evaporate.

However, this void is where true fulfillment begins. Eros thrives in these moments of wanting; it is through the dynamic tension between "wanting" and "having" that orgasmic energy can build and power individuals. Yet many spend their lives lamenting this scarcity—missing this key opportunity to tap into the erotic perfection that flourishes in moments of yearning. Karen Johnson, A.H. Almaas's co-author of *The Power of Divine Eros*, explains this further: "When we allow ourselves to fully experience our wanting, and we trust that the wanting itself has the intelligence to reveal the pure energy of desire that underlies it, we get a taste of what it's like to feel love and desire as a unified force."[7]

Letting go of the idea that it's either "my pleasure or their pleasure" in the bedroom and releasing the notion that showing how much desire lies within is "giving up our power," the sexual warfare game stops and people can start generously relating to each other as divine lovers. The limiting roles of "giver & receiver," "purchaser & commodity," and even "masculine & feminine" fall away and the heart of eros reveals its truth: receiving is giving the opportunity for another to express their divine gift, and giving is receiving the intimate vulnerability of another's desire.

---

[7] Almaas, A.H., and Karen Johnson. *The Power of Divine Eros*. Boston: Shambala, 2013. 76. Print.

A.H. Almaas elaborates in *Divine Eros*, "Experiencing satisfaction is also giving satisfaction. And by giving satisfaction, we experience satisfaction. The love is so dynamic that there is no difference between giving and taking, between love and desire. This is what true divine love means."[8] This "true divine love" is the fastest way to erotic fulfillment and sexual decommodification. When we connect to the spirit of eros, consumption becomes consummation and commerce becomes communion. Every action becomes a prayer and an offering in the service of love. Sexuality opens the door to eros but is not a replacement for it. Learning how to infuse the negatively-charged arena of sexuality with eros can teach one to adapt it to other realms. However, this requires a collective overhaul of the current system of sexual education.

---

8 Almaas 42.

the miseducation of sex: abstinence, pornography, and romance

Because of our society's confusion surrounding sex and eros, the primary sources of sexual acculturation—abstinence, pornography, and romance—provide a two-dimensional view of sexuality. To be clear, there is nothing inherently wrong with abstinence, pornography, or romance. But if they are the *sole* socially acceptable contexts for sexual behavior, people can easily feel confused, ashamed, angry, unfulfilled, and entitled when their lives don't match the "lessons" contained within each system.

The fact that abstinence, pornography, and romance are the three reigning containers for sexuality reflects society's conflicting fear and fascination with sex. Through abstinence, we learn to repress sexuality and regard it as a temptation to overcome to maintain virtue. Through pornography, we learn that we must be sexual gods and that success as humans rests on some nearly impossible version of virility. And through romance, we learn to reserve sex only for that one special snowflake who will rescue us from our loneliness.

With three such disparate, yet constrictive, views of sexuality—not to mention the limiting binary gender roles that come with each one—it's no wonder why embarking on sexual and erotic awakening requires such courage.

abstinence

Abstinence, while an appropriate choice at times, teaches that moral virtue rests in the ability to refrain from sex until marriage or to abstain from it altogether in the case of a clerical life. This creates a wedge between natural or innocent erotic desire and the desire to be ethical, upstanding citizens of society. In abstinence-based education, one is not taught to be the arbiter of her own sexuality, but instead is subject to the rules forced upon her by a system of ideology—religion, government, patriarchy, traditionalism, etc. These so-called "protectors" of virtue succeed mostly in disempowering and often abusing those they claim to protect.[9] People who stray from abstinence's tenets risk isolation, ridicule, and even banishment from social communities. In many places around the world, sexual "deviance" is a criminal offence punishable by imprisonment or even death, with women, people of color, homosexuals, trans, non-binary, and/or intersex people receiving the brunt of these punishments. The withholding of sexual information does not create freedom from desire—it fosters a system of oppression, where curiosity is criminalized and one fears to ask, "What do *I* want?"

In the U.S. many proclaim themselves the "defenders of free thought," but the government's spending habits demon-

---

[9] Two ultra-conservative communities that have recently come under fire for sexual abuse amongst its religious leaders are Catholics and Hasidic Jews. These groups place hard restrictions on sexual behavior, including the behavior of its clerics, as in the case of abstinent-for-life priests. More can be found at these resources:
Butt, Riazat. "Archbishop Links Priestly Celibacy and Catholic Sex Abuse Scandals." *The Guardian*. 11 March 2010. Web. 1 June 2016.
Otterman, Sharon, and Ray Rivera. "Ultra-Orthodox Jews Shun Their Own for Reporting Child Sexual Abuse." *New York Times*. 9 May 2012. Web. 1 June 2016.

strate a strong preference for abstinence-only education. Attorney Dana Northcraft notes, "In 1981, Congress passed the Adolescent Family Life Act (AFLA), which provided federal funds to programs that were designed to 'promote self-discipline and other prudent approaches' to adolescent sex. In other words, the purpose was to teach minors not to have sex. In 1997, Congress passed additional conservative legislation through the attachment of restrictions onto welfare reform legislation that would give matching grants to programs teaching abstinence until marriage as the preferable behavior."[10]

The use of abstinence-only education, a method for controlling sexual behavior, stems from the fear of sexuality and erotic power. Most people don't want to deal with sexuality in their own lives and hesitate to face it in their children. Anger covers embarrassment as adults scold young kids who have stumbled upon an adult channel or been caught "playing doctor." Children are taught to watch out for a variety of boogeymen predators: pedophiles, STDs, unwanted pregnancy, etc. But fear is the real predator. The fear-based methods and avoidance techniques taught in abstinence-only education normalize victim blaming and slut shaming.

What abstinence has the opportunity to teach us are the skills of discipline and discernment. Of course people want to protect their children. It is perhaps *not* always in our best interest to have sex with everyone, especially as a means of preventing unwanted pregnancy or STDs. Children learn that a

---

[10] Northcraft, Dana, M. "A Nation Scared: Children, Sex and the Denial of Humanity." *Journal of Gender, Social Policy & the Law.* 12.3 (2011): 501–502. Web. 1 June 2016.

sexual touch from adults is not appropriate. But in order to speak up and say "No," young people must feel empowered and unashamed of their "Yes." Shielding, shaming, and projecting sexual shadows onto children are not effective approaches. Teaching kids how to negotiate boundaries, declare consent, explore their desire, and practice safe sex can set free the innate erotic intelligence within their bodies and guide them on the journey to a healthy relationship with sexuality and eros.

pornography

A direct descendent from the culture of abstinence is the world of pornography. Carl Jung is credited with the maxim, "What you resist not only persists, but will grow in size."[11] So the denial of sexuality through abstinence-only education has set the stage for a hyper-realistic, pseudo-sexuality born out of the addictive need to quench a forbidden thirst. To clarify, we are not defining pornography as merely watching people have sex on-camera or masturbating to naked pictures. In this case, pornography refers to Audre Lorde's definition as "plasticized sensation—a direct denial of the power of the erotic, for it represents the suppression of true feeling [and] emphasizes sensation without feeling."[12]

The formula for conventional heterosexual pornography usually begins with a man and woman meeting, continues with

---
11 Though a citation of this widely attributed quote has yet to be found directly in Jung's collected works, it is an accurate reflection of his psychological philosophy, specifically around the shadow. A variation of the quote is attributed to him in Rhonda Byrne's controversial book on the law of attraction, *The Secret*.
12 Lorde, 53.

him penetrating her with very little foreplay and her screaming in ecstasy as he pounds endlessly into her vagina, and ends when he ejaculates. This representation of sex is not only considered the norm, but is considered by many to be the epitome of sexual success. There is usually very little connection and a *lot* of performance. If spectators can learn to view conventional porn as what it really is, entertainment, then this formula isn't really a problem. **However, since general willingness to engage in frank conversations around sexuality and seek proper education is almost non-existent, what is meant as entertainment becomes education. This is the "pornification" of sex. And this "pornification" is based on a system primarily funded by men, directed by men, and targeted at men.**

Author Ian Kerner sums up the internalization of the male-centric sexual *status quo* in his book, *She Comes First*: "The male orgasm/ejaculation is enshrined in our culture's definition of sex. The male orgasm presages the denouement of the sex act, regardless of where a woman is in the process of sexual response and irrespective of her innate biological capacity to experience multiple orgasms. The male orgasm is the signifying event that defines what comes before, as well as after."[13]

Also entrenched in pornification is the objectification and fetishization of humanity, particularly people of color and queer-gendered people. Most consumers of porn are trained to pay for a commodity rather than for human connection. Categories—She-Men, Black, Asian, Big Girls, Big Titties, etc.—reduce people to a group of body parts and create a cul-

---
13 Kerner, Ian. *She Comes First*. New York: HarperCollins Publishers, 2004. 34. Print.

ture of sexual privilege, with sex on demand available at the click of a button. Of course, many people are attracted to specific physical attributes, but to reduce someone to *only* that part inhibits the potential for eros and intimacy in sex.

The scripts and formulas that dominate conventional pornography, coupled with its role as one of the primary sources of sex education, create a constrictive box around authentic desire and relating. As a result, men and women come to sex starving for the fruits of eros, yet resort to a sort of genital-based friction in an attempt to feel *something*, never realizing that their unfettered *aliveness* is the true erotic nourishment they seek.

The porn industry boasts several billion dollars a year, and it is clear that porn is not going to disappear. And to be fair, depicting sex through visual media is nothing new. From the ancient tantric temples in the Indian city of Kujaraho to the Shunga woodblock prints from Japan's Edo period to the works of nineteenth century Hungarian artist Mihály Zichy, sex has been the fascination of countless artists for thousands of years with the female form as muse in many cases.

It is no coincidence that Gustave Courbet, French Realist, entitled his iconic painting of a woman's vulva, *L'Origine du Monde* (The Origin of the World). Venetian Renaissance painter, Jacopo Tintoretto, also captured the feminine's role in the formation of our universe in his piece, *The Origin of the Milky Way*. Here, the Greek Goddess Hera spills forth milk from her breasts, creating the stars. For thousands of years, artists, poets, and mystics have equated the power of eros with the sexual, and a woman's body often becomes the entrance to that world.

One could argue that these were the creations of artists expressing their craft. But in their time, many people believed that they were worth banning or destroying because they were "vulgar," "tacky," or "immoral." Modern cultural definitions of "ethical" and "tasteful" all too often criticize sexual expression from different historical and cultural contexts as unacceptable. While it is almost guaranteed that what works for one person will not work for another, to denigrate, slander, or prohibit anything can easily result in shame, secrecy, and shadow-archetype expressions of desire and emotional needs—all of which tend to create more harm than not.

Clearly there is a need that is fulfilled by graphic depictions of sex and, moreover, when understood it can support a healthy relationship to eros. There's nothing wrong with watching people have sex or engaging in a live chat with a sex worker as long as she is there of her own volition. Judgmental, sex-negative perspectives may push the pendulum back towards abstinence. So how does one fulfill this need for sexual exploration and fantasy while also fostering intimacy and connection?

The answer lies less in *what* is consumed (though this does have an impact) and more on *how* it is consumed. The senses can be trained to work in favor of eros, and the choice of what to view will often begin to subsequently shift. That is when the pornification of sex stops and direct relationship with what is viewed begins—an experience called "erotic voyeurism."[14]

The distinction between pornification and erotic voyeurism ultimately lies in the question posed earlier: *Am I using my*

---

14 Holdorf, Candice. "Pornography vs. Erotic Voyeurism." *The Orgasmic Life*. 3 July 2013. Web. 1 June 2016.

sexuality as a means to become more present and self-aware based on my desire, or am I reacting out of craving and using sexuality as a means to numb and escape reality?

In the past few years, there has been a rise in websites and literature that foster a more erotically voyeuristic view of sex. Photographer and filmmaker Clayton Cubitt's video art series, "Hysterical Literature," and websites like GentlemenHandling.com (which has unfortunately suspended its creation of new content) and Cindy Gallop's MakeLoveNotPorn.tv showcase real people instead of actors,[15] performing real sex acts based on their authentic, in-the-moment desire. Feminist porn companies such as Sensate Films, Feck, Bright Desire, and Feminist Porn Network, just to name a few,[16] not only feature female writers, directors, and producers who create content based on feminist values, but also work to ensure that the performers are ethically treated through fair wages (sometimes including residuals—a far cry from the conventional porn model), safe working conditions, and an emphasis on doing what feels good for the *performer*, rather than adhering to a script. And let's not forget legendary porn stars Nina Hartley, Annie Sprinkle, and the late Candida Royalle, who each pioneered content that not only entertained, but also educated and invited viewers to open the door to their own sexual curiosities.

These sites, companies, and educators reintroduce eros back into porn using three principles: desire, vulnerability,

---

[15] With the exception of Cubitt's "Literature," which does include a porn actress, a comedian, a performance artist, and a burlesque dancer. However, the performers in "Literature" aren't acting in the project.

[16] More information on feminist porn sites can be found at www.feministpornawards.com.

and participation. We see desire in the performers—specifically the women—and can feel their genuine orgasms build, rumble, and quake, rather than settle for the plasticized fake screams so often found in conventional porn. We see vulnerability within the scenes—the performers aren't surgically enhanced starlets or abnormally endowed he-men. They are gorgeously flawed humans and their interactions are rife with giggles, spills, unexpected shrieks, and unfettered aliveness. We see participation in how the videos are staged and categorized. The viewer isn't merely passive, but invited to step in, feel the humanity of the performers, and self-reflect. Scenes aren't reduced to objectifying names based on race, gender, or sexual orientation, but *feeling* words like romping, gushing, cozy, yummy, succulent, and friendly, as demonstrated by MakeLoveNotPorn.tv.

romance

One especially powerful aspect of erotic voyeurism is that it showcases unabashed feminine desire that breaks the bounds of how female sexuality is typically portrayed in the media. Mainstream media is inundated with trailers for the latest rom-coms or so-called "women's" magazines with headlines like "How to Snag a Husband" or "10 Sex Moves That Will Keep Him Satisfied." So it is rarely even hinted that women might actually *want* sex outside of a heterosexual, monogamous, marriage-bound relationship. Or, if one is having sex "illicitly," as in affairs, the couple's actions are justified only as long as they are "in love." **The linking of sexuality as acceptable only if you are "in love" or potentially on the way to being "in love" is known as the romantification of sex.**

Romance parallels abstinence and pornography in that sexuality is used as a substitute for getting some sort of erotic need met. In abstinence, this need is connected to morality. In porn, it is connected to power. In romance, the need is connected to one's lovability in pursuit of the experience of "being in love" and, according to the stereotype, subsequently entrapping "Mr. Right" in a long-term, monogamous partnership, a.k.a. marriage. The problem with this is twofold: first, it teaches women to voluntarily put up insurmountable boundaries around sex—why waste time with anyone who isn't "Mr. Right"?—in a society that already represses female sexuality. Second, it trains her to use her body and desire solely in service of potential partnerships—not for her own pleasure or benefit. Sex then becomes a commodity rather than an autonomous and empowered expression of her truth.

From a young age, girls are taught the fairytale plotline for relationships: be beautiful and nice, meet a hot guy, become a damsel in distress, and when the hot guy saves you, marry him. Romance-based stories aimed at adult women aren't that much different, though there may be a sexual caper or two thrown into the mix. But nowhere in that narrative do women empower themselves by discovering their own erotic truths.

Robert Moore and Douglas Gillette's seminal book on masculine archetypes, *King, Warrior, Magician, Lover: Rediscovering the Archetypes of the Mature Masculine*, describes the immature masculine's role within the fairy tale dynamic: "In the medieval legends about heroes and damsels, we are seldom told what happens once the hero has slain the dragon and married the princess. We don't hear what happened in their marriage, because the Hero, as an archetype, doesn't know what to do with the Princess once he's won her. He doesn't know what to do when things return to normal."[17]

Discovering the extraordinary pleasure within this "normalcy" is the heart of erotic relating. It is quite easy to "feel the passion" when lovers are in the crisis of "will we or won't we get together." But deeper work occurs within the day-to-day renewal of erotic presence. This kind of relating sets the stage for relationships to be evolutionary containers of growth, rather than dusty trophies to cling to. Then partners can transform into glorious mirrors of each other's souls, instead of coping mechanisms for assuaging the discomforts arising from the void of one's insecurities.

Romantification robs sex of eros through its adherence to *logos*-based formulas for how and when to engage sexually. In fact, a book literally called *The Rules*[18] teaches women the supposed ins and outs of proper sexual behavior for the purpose of finding a husband. Conversely, men are taught "the rules" for how to "pick up"[19] women—a system based on men get-

---

17 Moore, Robert, and Douglas Gillette. *King, Warrior, Magician, Lover: Rediscovering the Archetypes of the Mature Masculine.* San Francisco: HarperOne, 2013. Loc 617. Kindle.

18 Fein, Ellen, and Sherrie Snyder. *The Rules: Time-Tested Secrets to Capture the Heart of Mr. Right.* New York: Warner Book, 1995. Print.

19 The "Pick-Up Artist" and "Seduction" communities have been around since the 1970's and were recently made popular by journalist Neal Strauss in his book,

ting laid while circumnavigating the relational aspects of interacting with a woman. Once again commodification governs sexuality, with society teaching women to hold the cards for sex and men to hold the cards for love.

The point is not to slam romance novels, fashion magazines, Disney fairy tales, or rom-com movies. They can be fun when viewed as entertainment—just like porn. And one thing that romance does right is emphasize the need for heart to genital connection. But connecting heart to genitals doesn't always mean being "in love" or "on the road to marriage." It simply refers to bringing the principle of eros back into sex. Empathy. Presence. Compassion. Unconditional Love. All of these are possible in any iteration of sex—a one-night stand, a BDSM scene, or a thirty-year marriage.

a new education

Scrambling to make sense of the meager sexual knowledge available, women get caught between innate, carnal passions and the moral code dictated by society. But when the erotic is restored to sexuality, abstinence, pornography, and romance are simply three tools on an extended tool belt teaching us about discernment, erotic voyeurism, and heart to genital connection, respectively. This new, integrated perspective

---

The Game. Pick-Up Artists claim to teach techniques and strategies for men to seduce and gain sexual access to women. Their techniques include "negging," which is giving a woman a backhanded compliment in order to lessen her confidence and "pawning," which is discarding or trading a woman to another pick-up artist as a display of status. These communities have been heavily criticized for being misogynistic and for promoting male sexual entitlement and violence.

on sex liberates and invites eros to take its rightful place in people's lives. We no longer see the sex depicted in the media as the rule but as a reference for deeper inquiry.

discovering eros
through archetypes

Carl Jung, the creator of modern archetypal psychology, wrote, "One does not become enlightened by imagining figures of light, but by making the darkness conscious."[20] This definition of enlightenment isn't about spiritual superiority, but refers to its original meaning: to remove blindness and shine a light upon the darkness.

This definition also works in accordance with Carl Jung's philosophy regarding the shadow, which, in psychological terms, is the unacknowledged part of ourselves repressed into our unconscious. These shadow parts don't go away but work surreptitiously to get their needs met, even if it is to the detriment of our health and growth. Jungian psychologists believe that "shining a light" upon the shadow—enlightenment—leads to integration, healing, and spiritual maturation. The point is to stop vilifying the shadow and acknowledge its existence so that its wisdom may be integrated into the conscious. Jung himself said, "I must have a dark side also if I am to be whole."[21] This wholeness comes not from chasing spiritual perfection but by dropping into the balanced totality

---

[20] Jung, Carl. "The Philosophical Tree." Alchemical Studies (*Collected Works of Carl Jung, Vol. 13*). Ed. and trans. G. Adler and R.F.C. Hull. Princeton, NJ: Princeton University Press, 1967. 265–66. Print.

[21] Jung, Carl. "Problems of Modern Psychotherapy." *Modern Man in Search of a Soul.* Trans. W.S. Dell and Cary F. Baynes. New York: Harcourt Harvest, 1933. 35. Print.

of the human experience; in turn, everything is an opportunity for awakening.

One tool to guide the investigation of bringing the shadow into light is the exploration of archetypes. As stated in the introduction, Caroline Myss describes archetypes as "dynamic living forms of energy that are shared in many people's thoughts and emotions, across cultures and countries—these patterns, often ancient in origin, populate our minds and lives in ways that affect us deeply."[22] In *King, Warrior, Magician, Lover*, Moore and Gillette present a similar definition of archetypes, adding that they are "made up of instinctual patterns and energy configurations probably inherited genetically throughout the generations of our species."[23]

Moore and Gillette also cite a prominent Jungian theory. "In every man there is a feminine subpersonality called the Anima, made up of feminine archetypes. And in every woman there is a masculine subpersonality called the Animus, made up of masculine archetypes. To a greater or lesser degree, moreover, all human beings can access the archetypes. We do this, in fact, with our interrelating with one another."[24] So even though this book focuses on traditionally "feminine" archetypes, these archetypes live within people of all genders.

Archetypes provide a blueprint to the unifying power of eros. Humans as a species are inexorably linked. Every human is operating within the same psycho-emotional program in the form of archetypes. There's no escaping the Rock Star, the

---

22 Myss, 6.
23 Moore and Gillette 217.
24 Moore and Gillette 241.

Serial Killer, and the Dunce, bec~~
every person, and only by softening to ~~
eration happen. Archetypes help to put lan~~
scious patterns and "shine the light" on how th~~
can disconnect one from her erotic essence if they rema~~
egated to the shadows.

Eros includes it all—the dark, the light, and everything in between. The study of archetypes within the sexual and erotic provides a safe and conscious way to explore this spectrum and sets the stage for enlightenment rooted in the intelligent, integrated, and universal wisdom emanating from mature expressions of the feminine.

erotic initiation

We are about to embark on a journey like no other. We must be willing to enter the fire of transformation and let that blinding light reveal our essence. It is a journey into eros through the gateway of sexuality. It is a shamanic descent into the feminine heart of darkness with archetypes as our spiritual healers. It is *la petite mort*[25] for the soul.

As we step into these women's worlds, we must be willing to look beyond perceived differences and connect to the archetypal humanity woven into our collective unconscious. As we explore these women, I invite you to consider these questions:

- Where do I see myself reflected in this archetype?
- Where do I *not* see myself reflected in this archetype?
- What do I love about this archetype?
- What do I hate about this archetype?
- What do I fear about this archetype?
- How do I judge and/or punish myself for being like this archetype?
- How do I judge and/or punish myself for *not* being like this archetype?
- What does this archetype express that I want more of in my life?
- How can I love this archetype within myself?

---

[25] Translated from French, it means "the little death." *La petite mort* is a common euphemism for "orgasm."

- What would my life look like if I embraced this archetype?

By asking ourselves each of these questions and holding the answer with gentleness and curiosity, we open the portal of our unconscious to potential reintegration with these archetypes and pave the path to heal from the spiritual trauma that has afflicted us ever since our mythological banishment from Eden. Certain Latin cultures refer to a kind of spiritual affliction known as *susto*—which requires a shaman-led ritual in order for one to be reunited her soul.[26] This book serves as a similar ceremonial bridge for us to reclaim our relationship to eros. Our fragmented souls have lived in shame as fallen beings, split from our divinely human erotic essence. We've been unconscious participants in the war between heaven and earth, forgetting that it is through their union that we come to know love. This journey asks us to reunite with our erotic selves and return to the Garden of Innocence, while at the same time recognizing that we cannot do this alone. We are all each other's spiritual midwives as we give birth and are birthed into the age of eros.

Moore and Gillette argue that in order to align with the mature expression of ourselves, some part of ourselves must die—but with this death comes power: "Effective, transforma-

---

26 Literally translated from Spanish as "fright." Commonly refers to a culture-bound, psychosomatic illness found in the Hispanic populations of North and Central America. In traditional folk medicine, it refers to the separation of one's soul from their physical selves due to a shocking or frightening experience and often requires a ritual or ceremony in order to be healed. More recently, it refers specifically to the anxiety and/or depression one may experience when he or she cannot live up to the cultural expectations that come with adhering to traditional gender roles.

tive initiation absolutely slays the Ego and its desires in its old form to resurrect it with a new, subordinate relationship to a previously unknown power or center."[27]

How far are we willing to go to know this power? Methodist minister, William Booth, is credited with the wise axiom, "The greatness of a man's power is the measure of his surrender." Surrender is the ultimate act of faith—there are no roads, no maps, and no rules. All that is required is a resounding "yes" and a willingness to listen into the void of our erotic yearning—what Joseph Campbell calls "bliss" or "the *deep sense of being in it* and doing what the *push* is out of your own existence."[28] The door is open and the heroine's journey awaits. Let the initiation begin.

---

27 Moore and Gillette 180.
28 Campbell, Joseph, Phil Cousineau, and Stuart L. Brown. *The Hero's Journey: Joseph Campbell on His Life and Work (The Collected Works of Joseph Campbell)*. Centennial ed. Novato, CA: New World Library, 2003. 217. Print.

PART TWO

initiation

> *Woman, especially her sexuality, provides the object of endless commentary, description, supposition. But the result of all the telling only deepens the enigma and makes woman's erotic force something that male storytelling can never quite explain or contain.* ~ Peter Brooks

the virgin archetype
INNOCENCE, AUTONOMY

> *Perhaps our eyes need to be washed by our tears once in a while, so that we can see life with a clearer view again. ~ Alex Tan*

The Virgin Archetype uses her erotic energy to breathe new life into every moment. She maintains her independence from the stories, beliefs, and systems that do not serve her. Many approach life believing our wounded narratives of the past and fears/expectations of the future; however, the Virgin removes these filters from our eyes so we may witness life with childlike innocence. It's rare for us to sit squarely in the center of the present, and this is no more true than in the realms of the sexual and the erotic. We may fear exposing ourselves to new people because of past heartbreak. Or we might be so caught up in protecting our fragile egos that we focus on impressing a new lover rather than simply feeling her and accepting her as she is right now. Or we may see life through our resentments and collect evidence to prove how miserable we are.

In *Sacred Contracts*, Caroline Myss references the term "virgin forests," i.e., a new land that we have yet to explore or see.[29] Since every moment is a moment that we have yet

---
29 Myss, 421.

to explore or see, we can tap into this quality of innocence no matter how many times we may *think* we've actually seen it.

The modern interpretation of the Virgin is a woman who has yet to have penile/vaginal intercourse. However, this is a surface-level and culturally twisted version of the Virgin used to confine the wild feminine. According to this skewed definition of Virgin, a woman's value is largely based on her sexual exploits, or lack thereof. To "win" or "buy" a virgin is a high prize—if she is suspected of having sex outside the bonds of marriage, she is depreciated as "spoiled goods."

In her book *Willful Virgin*, Marilyn Frye challenges our modern definition of Virgin: "The word 'virgin' did not originally mean a woman whose vagina was untouched by any penis, but a free woman, one not betrothed, not bound to, not possessed by any man. It meant a female who is sexually and hence socially her own person. In any universe of patriarchy, there are no Virgins in this sense."[30]

In the nascent years of Christianity, a woman's vow of chastity predominantly had less to do with her devotion and more to do with her freedom. As consecrated virgins, they could escape government gender laws, were free to lead and preach in their own communities, and often dressed in men's garb. That is until the end of the third century, when chaste women were murdered, raped, or forced into prostitution. Eventually, these women were written out of biblical history altogether.

---

30 Frye, Marilyn. "Willful Virgin or Do You Have to Be a Lesbian to Be a Feminist?" *Willful Virgin: Essays in Feminism*. Freedom, CA: The Crossing Press, 1992. 133. Print.

When we take this definition of "virgin as autonomous" beyond freedom from patriarchy and into the realm of sovereign spirit, we begin to imagine freedom from *all* thoughts, stories, and fears that bind us. Can you imagine delving deep into your own pure essence and bringing that to your everyday encounters? This is what it means to embody the Virgin archetype on the highest levels.

the shadow virgin

The Virgin has two major shadow manifestations: the Dunce and the Prude. The Dunce often appears in feminine form as the "blonde bombshell" who cannot figure out anything and is dependent upon others—usually men—for her survival. Often, her idiocy is a mask so she can avoid taking responsibility for her intelligence and can delegate to others the tasks she doesn't want to do.

The second shadow is the Prude or the "good girl" who doesn't dare begin the journey into "virgin territory." She fears her own erotic power and intensely guards her innocence. Yet she's actually the one caught up in the patriarchal belief that her value rests between her thighs. She has forgotten that her purity is present in all aspects of her life and is only hers to claim. It cannot be taken away from her.

integrated and shadow examples of the virgin

- Artemis: Greek Goddess of virginity, hunting, the

moon, wild things, and the natural environment.
- Athena: Greek Goddess of wisdom who never had a consort.
- Elizabeth I: "Virgin Queen" who ruled England for forty-four years without a husband.
- Hero: Character from Shakespeare's *Much Ado About Nothing* who demonstrated immense capacity for forgiveness and pure love, despite the injustice inflicted upon her by the patriarchal system.
- Marcella: Early Christian leader of noblewomen who had left their fortunes and taken a vow of chastity.
- Medeina: Lithuanian Goddess of the forest and animals. She was a huntress that refused to get married.
- Vestal Virgins: Roman priestesses and guardians of the Hearth who were emancipated from their fathers' rule, handled their own property, and were free to marry after thirty years of service.
- Virgin Mothers: Mary, Quan Yin, Virgin of Guadalupe, Isis, Chimalman—mother of Aztec god Quetzalcoatl, Boldogasszony—Hungarian Virgin Mother.
- Fairy Tale Princesses: Their sexual purity and "good girl" attributes seemingly make them "Princess material" (Prude shadow).
- Claire Standish: Molly Ringwald's role in *The Breakfast Club* (Prude Shadow).
- Roles often played by Marilyn Monroe (Dunce Shadow).

inviting the virgin into our lives

How do we invite the Virgin archetype into our everyday lives? We can start with slowing down and tapping into the senses. Rather than rushing through a bar of chocolate, look at it first. Notice the color, texture, smell, and feel it melting between the fingertips. Listen to it. Does it have a vibration? Many musicians experience synesthesia and can "see" through sound. Notice the sensation as it sits on the lips. Feel the watering in the mouth. Notice how desire rises in the belly. Place it on the tongue and again, simply feel and soften. Get to know *this bite of chocolate in this very moment*. It will never arrive again.

Once the Virgin awakens in our lives, we are capable of releasing the past, stopping our projections, and living in the present. All of these can lead to an increased capacity for pleasure, wonder, delight, joy, and forgiveness.

SLUT

I was a Virgin for a long time.

Perhaps you think
I mean
I took 21 years
To let a man Penetrate me,

Measuring
My Worthiness
By the diminishing inches
Of his Cock?

No.

I mean a Virgin
In a language long forgotten:
Lost in the ashes
Of burned witches

Or in the silenced vows
Of Brides of Christ,
Whose names were erased
In canonical Genocide.

I was a Virgin.

RECLAIMING EROS

A woman unto herself;
Whole; Unshackled; Owned by No One;
And in this way
We've always been Virgins.

Our Women's wisdom,
Written in our Mothers' bosom,
Survived the translation migration
From Page to Pyre.

Observe your Holy Rights.

Do I deserve to be attacked,
Unwritten from history,
Because I fucked my way
Through the Zodiac?

Keep your righteous indignation.
Your taunts and jeers
Only urge my Vestal Reclamation
And the resurrection of my Erotic Innocence.

We. Are. Coming.

So here I stand:
Palms stretched, legs spread,
Re-Virginized once more,
While making love to the Sacred Whore.

lilith

Her bare feet hit the dirt like a spellbound drummer. Possessed. Unapologetic. In perfect rhythm. In spite of the rocks, branches and other earthly protrusions that announced their presence with each piercing step, She heeded an otherworldly call to just keep going.

In fact, their existence did very little to slow Her down. Where She would normally waver in endurance, She discovered an untapped well of strength. Which was surprising, given Her intimate knowledge of the Steep Ravine Trail. A vertical nemesis that had kicked Her ass on several occasions.

She brazenly wore Her anger like a perfectly-tailored suit—despite the fact that Her *vêtements* consisted of nothing but a light blue hospital gown. But She wasn't focused on her garments.

She couldn't recall the origin of this anger. It simply fueled Her, like a gasoline reservoir, and it didn't seem to be burning off any time soon.

And yet, despite Her fiery largess, She didn't take more than three steps before the same possession and intensity running through Her feet suddenly forced them to a startling halt. She felt the cool, moist air intermingle with the sheer sweat glistening on Her face. The usual acoustic fray of chirping birds and foraging squirrels seemed to dissipate into an unspeakable hush. A circle of bay laurel shrub glowed dark green, thanks to a late seasonal shower. Within this abrupt intermission, She watched as an arm of distant fog silently extended its fingers towards Her.

She knew this exact place—or at least She thought She did. Of course, She knew it from the many times She'd rushed by it on Her jogs. But She'd rarely paid attention to any one particular spot. At least, not since She was fifteen, when Her silent meditations within the crag's hidden glades turned into extra hours working at the Safeway.

For the past twenty-two years, Her relationship with the mountain was simply professional: She ran, and it provided the terrain. Its once mysterious landscape, provoking Her boundaryless childhood imagination, had fallen upon jaded eyes and ears.

But today was different. She stood transfixed and found Herself wedged within that strange nexus which often accompanies *déjà vu*—familiarity and disquietude.

The sudden sound of voices murmuring and leaves crackling underfoot broke the silent spell. Even as they grew closer, She did not move. She stood transfixed until they were only a few yards away before ducking behind a large, stoic redwood.

She saw before Her two young girls, each around fifteen years old. One had a single, auburn braid descending down her petite back. She wore Mary Janes and a pale white baby doll dress, which in juxtaposition to her nearly translucent skin, accented her kelpie-like appearance.

The other girl sported a short, spiky cut with obsidian black roots and iced pink tips reminiscent of a frosted cupcake. She was dressed in all black: Doc Martens, jeans, leather jacket and a Pearl Jam T-shirt.

One could not have imagined an odder pair traversing the scandent ridge. Yet, despite their aesthetic differences, the two girls seemed quite at home with each other.

"This is it," said Braid Girl.

"It *is* special," replied Pink Tips.

"I thought you'd like it. Since it's far from the usual trails, there aren't usually a lot of people that come by—which means it's perfect for doing whatever you want without anyone bothering you."

Braid Girl led the way to the base of an enormous redwood tree, split by lightning. Inside the charred trunk lay a small patch of orange California poppies, newly in bloom thanks to the warm spring sun. The girls entered the trunk's cavity—which surrounded them on three sides—and brushed away some leaves as they settled into their clandestine nook. Pink Tips pulled out a plastic Ziploc bag and started rolling a joint.

Unclear as to why She was loitering, She kept Her rapt attention upon the teenagers.

Finally after a few minutes of silence, while Pink Tips put the finishing touches on the joint, Braid Girl looked at her and asked, "Eva?"

Pink Tips stopped and glanced over at her friend. "Yeah?"

"Do you ever wonder what you would be like if you were born somebody else?"

"I don't know," Eva answered. "Yeah, sometimes. Sometimes I think about what my life would look like if we'd stayed in Seoul when I was a baby."

"I'm not talking about if your life were different. I'm talking about if you were a different person entirely," Braid Girl clarified.

"Well, then," added Eva, "I guess I would be like somebody else. I mean, I guess it would depend on where I was born, ya know? What my parents were like? How much money we had?"

Braid Girl elucidated her question. "Yeah, but do you think your *soul* would want the same things? Like, even if you were, like, Princess Diana, or someone like that, would you still want to dye your hair and smoke weed? Does the part of you that likes those things change just because we have a different set of circumstances? Or would they just look different because of your upbringing? Maybe you'd choose a dress above the knee and drink lots of champagne—but what if the *core* desire that exists within Eva right now and Eva as Princess Diana was exactly the same?"

Taking a large toke off the joint, Eva held her breath for a few seconds, then began coughing and laughing at the same time.

"You think too much, kiddo," she said, smiling with affection.

"C'mon, I'm serious, though," Braid Girl replied. "Don't ya ever wonder, like, how much better off you'd be with parents who actually loved each other and had enough money to not have to worry about shit—but then maybe you'd realize that all this crap that we have going on in our lives would be the same stupid crap no matter how else our lives looked?"

"I don't know, Lily. Maybe it'd be the same stupid crap—but maybe at least we'd have better ways of dealing with it. Maybe we'd have more people to talk about it with. Life might be a lot nicer to deal with. Less bullshit, ya know? Where's this all coming from, anyway?"

"No place, really." Lily with the braid paused. After a moment, she added, "This place just seems to bring out the philosopher in me, I guess."

"Well," said Eva, holding out her hand, "I think you should take this J and enjoy being Lily as Lily right now, in this moment. That's what I think."

Lily took the joint between her thin fingers, effortlessly inhaled the pungent smoke and leaned back against the trunk. Eva scooted closer to her and leaned her back against the tree as well. A foggy gust blew through their forest cove, causing the flowering redwood branches to fall into a rustling dance, before settling back down. A thick, warm cloud of marijuana and reticence shrouded the girls once more.

She couldn't move. Intrigued by the scene unfolding before Her, She squatted a little lower in order to get a better view of the girls. Her curiosity trumped any embarrassment She may have felt if She got caught.

Breaking the silence, Lily's face lit up as she started chuckling to herself.

"What's so funny?" asked Eva.

"Oh, I was just thinking of Edgar; you know, the really skinny guy in gym class? Crazy-frizzy hair?"

"Yeah, I know," said Eva, sitting up with interest.

"Yeah, well, he tried to kiss me today."

"What!?" screamed Eva.

"Yeah," Lily continued through her laughter. "I mean, he's nice and all, but the dude actually came at me with most of his tongue already sticking out of his mouth. He looked like a hungry anteater or something."

Lily grabbed Eva's face and stuck out her tongue, mimicking the boy's movements as if it were out of some sort of horror film.

"Oh my fucking God, that's *disgusting*!" squealed Eva, resisting her advances but not completely pushing Lily off of her body. "Why did he try to kiss you?"

"I don't know. Desperation or something. He dropped his notebook in the hall after school, so I picked it up for him and told him I liked his shirt. Then he started telling me how nice I looked and all that and before I knew it he was attacking me with his face. I didn't want to be mean or nothing, but—I'm just not into him."

"Well, what are you into?" asked Eva, her sly tone hovering in the air like a two-day-old foil balloon.

Lily hesitated before answering, a little taken aback by her friend's directness—limbs and fingers still tangled in their joking embrace.

"I don't know. No one's ever asked and I've never really thought about it. Just trying to keep things even at home, ya know? But I can definitely say with 100% assurance that I am *not* into anteaters."

They laughed for a moment before the silence returned. Lily unwound herself from Eva and took another toke of the joint to fill the pregnant, nervous void swelling between their bodies.

Lily inhaled, and with her most courageous nonchalance, she asked, "What are you into?"

Without missing a beat, Eva replied, "Girls."

"What?" gasped Lily.

"Why? Is there something wrong with that?"

"No! No!" assured Lily. "It's just—I wish I had such certainty."

"Well what's uncertain?" asked Eva, leaning forward.

"What I want. What I like. I've never been outside California. I've barely been outside Novato."

"Well, all that changes in a few months." Eva trailed off as she eagerly reached for her back pocket. She retrieved a black wallet connected to a silver link chain attached to her jeans and pulled out a plastic card.

"Check it out. It finally came in the mail."

"Your Learner's Permit!" squealed Lily excitedly, grabbing the card.

"Yup. Soon I'll be able to drive us out of this shithole."

Lily studied the photo ID for a few seconds.

"Eun Hwa?" she asked curiously.

"My legal name," Eva replied. "But nobody except my mother calls me that. And only when she's pissed at me."

"Oh."

Eva quickly grabbed the photo from Lily's hands.

"Mothers," Eva said, trying to laugh off her embarrassment. Lily smiled to appease her friend but did not share the sentiment of maternal disciplinary strife.

"I bet your mom calls you by your full name all the time," teased Lily, hoping to ease her friend's discomfort.

"I don't know," said Eva. "My parents are too busy hating each other to worry about me. But, yeah, come to think of it, she kinda does yell at me a lot. I'm not the 'proper little daughter' she wanted. Doing things she can't understand. Back in New York, I used to escape to the Village. Ride the subway with butches and drag queens. They showed me that there were people who thought and felt just like me. They reminded me that I wasn't alone. I knew I liked girls from the time I was six. Little Suzie Goldberg in first grade. Fuck, that girl broke my heart."

Eva paused her speech to giggle at the memory of her elementary-school self torn to bits over her first lost love.

"Anyway," she continued, "so, yeah, girls. I like girls. I like the softer ones. The ones with a little more innocence."

"Yeah?" Lily asked, only then noticing that she'd been holding her breath.

"Yeah. They aren't afraid to show their emotions. They aren't afraid to let me know how they feel. They just kinda throw themselves at ya with total enthusiasm. Of course, it can get a little crazy sometimes—all melodrama and soap opera shit—but when a girl is just so innocent and sweet and totally loving everything I'm doing—man, there's nothing better on earth. So, yeah. That's what I'm into."

Eva looked over at Lily to see that she was staring intensely back at her. Like a thief caught in the act, Lily quickly turned her eyes down towards the ground.

Silence spread between them. Watching while Eva stuffed her ID in her wallet, Lily thought back on the fragments of her own mother. A golden curl here. A freckle there. Splintered shards that pieced together some forgotten remembrance. Like a cracked attic mirror.

"You ever read Rumi's poem 'The Guest House?'" Lily asked.

"I think I remember something about that," replied Eva, unsure where the conversation was going.

"It's how I remember my mother. She used to read me his poetry before I went to sleep."

Eva looked at her, the threads beginning to weave but not fully understanding the tapestry's meaning.

"She died when I was six. Cancer. An unexpected visitor. Closed down her guest house almost overnight."

"I'm sorry, Lily."

"Don't be," Lily soothed. "I've learned to let her go. Can't say the same for my pops though."

"Oh?"

Lily repetitively ran her fingers over the green-fringed tree trunk as she replied, "He'd rather stay drunk within her memory than face the sober pain of reality. Jameson is his lover now. I've never seen him with any other woman. I think it hurts too much."

"What does?"

"Letting himself feel."

"Feel what?"

"Love."

The girls looked over the horizon. The approaching fog beckoned to them, as if calling them out from their hiding place.

Eager to shift the energy, Lily began speaking again.

"Maybe he'll move on once I leave for college. He keeps talking about heading out into the open-plain anonymity of Kansas or Oklahoma. Somewhere where he can take the last vestiges of his love for mom and bury them with no human reminders marking the gravestone. I sorta wish that for him. I don't need anyone to take care of me. I'd rather he find peace in his solitude than be bound to me by some perceived obligation of fatherhood."

"That's—erm—big of you. I guess," Eva hesitantly replied.

Lily looked away with a shrug. Too ashamed to share the emotions encroaching on her stoic visage, she hid her face from Eva.

"You know, you're allowed to be pissed. Or hurt. Or sad. Or whatever."

Eva walked her fingers over to Lily until they rested on Lily's translucent hand.

"He might choose to be alone. But you don't have to be."

Lily turned her watery eyes upon Eva. The posturing and pretense of adolescence melted from them both and, for the first time, the two girls began to see each other.

As the crackling wave of their connection swelled, so did Lily's boldness. Finally she declared, "Eva, I have a confession."

"Yeah?" Eva inquired, intrigued by Lily's sudden proclamation.

"When you first moved here two months ago, I thought you were a stuck-up city kid who was going to beat me up or something."

Eva burst out laughing. "Haha! What?! What made you think that?"

"Well, you dye your hair and wear lots of black and didn't seem like you wanted to talk much to anyone. Plus, when I heard you were from New York City, I thought you had to be tough to survive a place like that. Like, you wouldn't take shit from anyone who got in your way."

Eva replied, "Yeah, well, I thought you were some weird, emo kid who had taken a vow of silence or something. Just this slight, sullen form slipping though the halls."

"Really?"

"Yeah, kinda. I mean, I didn't think there was anything *wrong* with you. You just seemed, I don't know, unapproachable."

"Oh."

"But I see now you're just like me," continued Eva. "Lone wolf. Needing little. Asking for less."

"Well," Lily said, "I'm glad Mr. Chung's science project forced us to work together then."

"And why is that?" asked Eva.

"Cuz now I know you."

"And what do you think?"

Lily answered, "Well, I think you're cool and not like the other kids who are all into themselves and how they look and sucking up to the teachers. And I think you're smart, like super smart, and I think you're pretty and—I like you. You're a good friend. I haven't really ever had a good friend before."

Eva blushed before smiling and in a surprisingly shy voice said, "Thank you." The silence crept in once more for a few seconds before Eva offered, "Do you want to know what I think about you?"

"Sure."

"Well, I think you're also smart and way too good for that shitty school we go to. In fact, I think you're too good for this town and your father and that you haven't really had the chance to shine as *you*. And—" Eva paused for a moment, not really sure she could go on.

"What?" asked Lily, aching to hear more.

"Well, I think you are soft. And sweet and innocent. And—exactly what I'm into."

Lily took a deep breath and smiled tightly. And still, she could not let herself fully release into the warm, yearning blood rushing through her.

"Thanks," she replied through her thin, taut lips. "I-I like you too. I think we'll be great friends." Lily averted her eyes back towards the landscape and shifted her weight away from Eva.

Dejected, Eva slumped back against the tree trunk and began to fumble in the front pocket of her leather jacket. She pulled out a candy sucker, removed the wrapper and shoved it in her mouth. She was glad to have something to sweeten the bitter taste.

From Her hiding place, She felt an unbearable magnetic pull towards the two young women. The sight of them, barely able to admit their desire for each other, was almost too much for Her to witness. Whatever ache they were experiencing seemed to be magnified twenty times inside of Her own heart. She felt the crushing weight inside Eva's chest, yet She also understood the fear and hesitancy within Lily.

Finally, after what seemed like an agonizing minute of silence, Lily looked over at Eva, determination in her eyes, and declared, "I trust you."

Eva paused before turning towards Lily. She settled into Lily's gaze once more, gathering her courage, and asked, "You trust me?"

"Yes," continued Lily. "And I want to feel you."

Eva continued to stare, stunned and not quite sure what to believe.

Lily decided to make her intentions clearer. Without breaking her gaze, she reached her small hand towards Eva's face, pulled the sucker out from her friend's mouth and slowly placed the fluorescent green candy on her own tongue.

As She watched Lily wrap her lips around the semi-melted sugar, the saccharine taste of green apple flooded Her own mouth and ran down Her body. It all suddenly made sense. The bare feet. The hospital gown. The waxy white strip surrounding Her left wrist. She lifted Her arm to look at the words typed out on the paper bracelet as a momentary chill gripped Her throat. The forty-something-year-old nurse's image floated back into Her memory. She held a glass vase containing a bouquet of marigolds that contrasted brightly against her pale blue scrubs.

"These are my mother's favorite," said the nurse. "Thought you might like them, too."

The nurse, a woman with a darker complexion, gold-painted fingernails and a southern drawl, placed the flowers on the table next to Her bed.

"Let me sing you a little something, sweet one. You know I was named after Ella Fitzgerald. *There's a somebody I'm longing to see/I hope that She, turns out to be/Someone who'll watch over me.*"

Without another thought, She leapt from Her hiding place and cried out, "Lily!"

Lily jerked her head up and looked in Her direction but stared as if seeing nothing.

"What's wrong?" Eva asked.

"I'm not sure." Lily replied. "Nothing, I suppose. I just—I don't know—felt something calling me."

"What? I didn't hear anything."

"No, not out there *per se*. Something *in* me, I guess. I don't know." Lily trailed off, feeling exposed and somewhat embarrassed.

"This place does seem to have special powers," Eva said, reassuring Lily that she understood. When she felt her friend soften, Eva cupped her hands around Lily's face and pulled it towards hers.

The soft receptivity of Eva's lips came as a remembered surprise to Her. She recalled the hard edges and Don't-fuck-with-me attitude Eva emanated when they first met twenty-two years ago. The juxtaposition of that memory and the current scene before Her made Her laugh. She looked down once more at the laminated hospital bracelet, a souvenir from Her own lost battle with cancer (as She would always be Her mother's daughter), silently reading Her name: Lilith Ann Gardener.

Like an extension of what was left of Her own body, Her younger self transmitted a direct, visceral experience into Her. She watched as young Lily surrendered onto the leafy ground and received Eva's delicate flicks of the tongue across her pink nipples. She watched as Eva lifted up the edges of Lily's baby doll dress and indulged in the scent of the moistening crease between her legs. She watched as Eva first inserted one finger. Two fingers. Then four. Into Lily's desperately hungry and formerly lonesome self.

Tears streamed down Her face as She remembered every note of that sensual symphony. *This moment*. In the final instants of Her passing, She had returned to this moment. The only time in Her life that Her heart had opened. The only time in Her life that She felt She could finally trust Herself. The only time in Her life that She had dared to hope for love.

And She knew, for young Lily, it would only be three weeks later that this hope would suddenly be replaced with vile hatred. Hatred for her life. Hatred for herself. Hatred for the privileged teenage boy who would kill Eva in a drunken joyride with his father's stolen Dodge Viper.

But no matter how cold and isolated Her thirty-seven years had been, She could not deny that She had known love. At least once. And for that, She was grateful.

Which is why She remained silent as Lily and Eva fell back down to earth, chests pressing into one another and holding on as if even God couldn't tear them apart. She knew She could not warn the doe-eyed teenager. She knew She could not insulate her from the inevitable pain. All She could do was release Lily into the already-lived future and forgive the rest.

Finally, Lily spoke. In a simple, matter-of-fact tone, she declared, "I love you. I think I will always love you."

Eva brightened at these words and rolled over to look her beloved in the face. She softly kissed Lily's forehead, her eyelids, her nose and finally rested on her lips, lingering for a few extra seconds.

They gazed at each other, radiant, shining and completely naked in every way. A chilly wind suddenly stirred them from their bliss and forced them onto their feet.

"The fog's coming in," Lily warned. "It'll get cold really fast."

Quickly, the two girls gathered their clothes and dressed. Eva and Lily giggled as they nearly slipped on a patch of yellow sourgrass before ambling down the mountain. As they disappeared in the distance, She could still see a pink blush nearly matching Eva's hair warming across Lily's cheeks.

She watched as the curtain of fog descended and quickly enveloped Her. Its misty molecules sank into Her membranes, separating Her skin from Her oneiric memories. She closed

Her eyes one last time and, with newfound trust, She fell backwards, vanishing into a cloud-arm embrace.

the whore archetype
INSPIRATION, INTEGRITY

> *Someone I loved once gave me a box full of darkness.*
> *It took me years to understand that this too, was a gift.*
> *~Mary Oliver*

The Whore Archetype is one of the most misunderstood patterns in our collective unconsciousness. Many associate the Whore with a woman who sells sexual favors for money or who simply has sex with many people. While this certainly can be one expression of the Whore, it is only one tiny aspect of her magnificent whole.

First, she teaches us lessons on personal integrity and boundaries. "Everyone has their price," as the saying goes. And the Whore invites us to discover what our price is. This inquiry goes much deeper than sex. She asks us to examine how much of our creativity, energy, talents, ideas, and self-expression we are willing to sell. Many are willing to give up their outspoken natures and traveling spirit for a secure paycheck and fifty years in a cubicle. Others will gladly sell their true beliefs and purchase false dogma for a government position.

Returning to sex, many courtesans are quite content with offering their bodies for sex in exchange for money, gifts, and not having to work an office job. Is the courtesan any less moral than the woman who would sell her fidelity to one man—even if she did not love him—for fiscal and domestic security? What is in integrity for one person may not be for the other and vice versa. The Whore challenges us to know our integrity and to set those boundaries as they arise.

Etymologically, the word "whore" comes from the Proto-Indo-European "qar," which serves as a base for many words meaning "lover." "Qar" is linked to the Proto-Germanic word "khoraz," which means "one who desires" as well as to the Sanskrit word "kama" (as in Kama Sutra), the Hindu god of love. Therefore, the Whore has a direct relationship with her passion and often uses those desires as a guide on her journey to love.

As a complement to our highest purpose, the Whore offers inspiration and healing to all who connect with her erotic power. Again, erotic not necessarily as sexual, but erotic as divine creative force. She knows exactly how to "seduce" genius from us; when we feel a lack of our own creative genius, we can plug into her infinite resources anytime and draw upon her abundance.

There are a great many sex workers who choose their work because they are called to heal through the sexual arts. They echo the temple prostitutes from ancient Greece, Rome, India, Asia Minor, and Central and South America who used their bodies as inspirational conduits to the Divine.

The Whore also offers the rare opportunity for the masculine to surrender. According to many neo-tantric philosophies, the masculine is typically the "unwavering spaceholder" while the feminine tumbles in wild, ecstatic chaos within his solid structure. Yet to confine any gender within a set of fixed traits is to rob that gender of its richness and range.

The Whore represents a more "penetrative" version of feminine energy. She pierces the underbelly of our psyches (where our shadows often lie) and reveals the creative treasures within them. She holds presence and invites all of us—including the masculine—to relinquish our vigilance, while exposing our deepest vulnerabilities. These qualities mirror the holding aspects of the Mother archetype, but they differ because the Whore can—unlike the Mother—connect as a consort with the masculine in the sexual realm.

the shadow whore

The primary shadow of the Whore archetype is the Sellout. This is someone who will do anything for a price. She has no sense of her own boundaries or integrity and essentially loses herself in others. She also does not know her own worth and frequently undercharges for her services—something we see often in the healing arts where alternative therapies such as acupuncture, reiki, and intuitive coaching are systematically undervalued. In *Sacred Contracts*, Caroline Myss describes the Whore/Prostitute as one who "dramatically embodies and tests the power of faith."[31] When we begin to lose faith in ourselves and in the inherent goodness of the universe, we start "selling out" in order to preserve our physical and egoic security. This eventually erodes our moral compass if

---
31 Myss, 118.

we begin accepting money from people who hurt others or do work that is in direct opposition to the ethics that we ostensibly hold dear.

The Sellout forgets her inherent abundance and lives in a state of constant fear that she will lose whatever is most precious to her. We've all seen movie stars turn into "attention whores" and perform in eye-rolling infomercials and reality TV shows out of extreme greed or fear of losing the spotlight. We've seen artists again and again sell the rights to their *oeuvres* to the highest paying producer-pimps. And yes, there are many starving addicts, both men and women, willing to sell sex to survive the pain of living.

integrated and shadow examples of the whore

- Aspasia: Ancient Greek prostitute who owned many of the brothels in Athens.
- Dakinis: Tantric healers who used their bodies—often sexually—as channels for healing and awakening.
- Freya: Nordic earth goddess of fertility; unafraid of her sexual power.
- Innana: Mesopotamian goddess whose houses of worship were associated with temple whores.
- Mary Magdalene: Prostitute according to some accounts; the feminine counterpart to Jesus according to Christian dogma.
- Muses: Nine Greek goddesses who ruled over various

aspects of the arts and sciences, offering inspiration and a place to plug into creative genius.
- Rahab: Biblical whore who lived in Jericho and helped the Israelites capture the city.
- Sexual surrogates: Modern-day professionals who heal psychological trauma using methods including physical sexual contact; dramatized in *The Sessions*.
- Shamanic Healers: People who utilize their bodies—either through physically or psychedelically-induced trances—to translate messages from hidden or subconscious sources. These people work to bring one to enlightenment through the path of darkness.
- Vivian Ward: Julia Robert's character in *Pretty Woman*; Whore with a Heart of Gold.
- Fame Whores: People—usually who have had a moment of fame—who are consistently selling their faces, bodies, and names as a "brand" simply to make money or remain in the spotlight (Sellout Shadow).
- Faust: Character from German legends who sells his soul for unlimited knowledge (Sellout Shadow).
- Certain government officials who sell their votes on important legislation to whichever group or lobbyist contributes the most to their campaign (Sellout Shadow).

inviting the whore into our lives

Invite the Whore archetype by asking the question, "What do I want and what am I willing to give up in exchange for it?" There is nothing wrong with profiting from our work, but we must clarify our boundaries if we are to stay in integrity. And profiting doesn't necessarily mean money—it could encompass power, fame, security, love, adventure, personal evolution, or any other host of things. The trick is to draw from an internal sense of fulfillment rather than react to externalized pressure and fears.

Let us embrace the Whore and allow her to share her wisdom in sacred commerce. Let this archetype challenge us to experiment and discover the landscape of our own integrity. She wants us to liberate her from her status as a sub-human member of society and to renounce the pejorative nature of her name. "Whore" may be a derogatory word for a woman who has sex with many people, but the Whore archetype asks us to cast off that shame and celebrate our sexual and erotic powers—for these are the forces that galvanize and seduce us to our greatest awakening and purpose.

in the garden

Jesus sits with me under the apple tree
Lapping honey from my left hand.
With the right, I pluck *pommes*
To feed my immaculate hunger.

"What is it about you that I love," he wonders,
"That the rest of the world has forgotten?
Why did I ever give you up
For a bloody scepter of glory?"

At this, I toss my wild hair back
And laugh with the primordial roar of the ancients.
Sunshine glows on my virgin face
As branches cast shadows on my open thighs.

"Well," I say, "perhaps one day, (when you are
Bold enough to rip yourself off that cross),
We can head back to my porch for everlasting
Sweet tea and eternal peach pie."

Sadness rests in his starving eyes, for he knows
That until his name is forgotten and humanity hums with
The knowledge of holy fruit, he is entangled
In my vines—a tongue's length away from Paradise.

magdalena

Desirée pulled her blue Honda into the icy driveway of the Harlingen, Texas apartment complex on a frigid 29°F afternoon. The holiday season was in full swing, even though it was only two days after Thanksgiving. White Christmas lights were strung along the trees that lined the sidewalk. Evergreen wreaths swathed in scarlet and gold hung like decorative door-knockers in the entryway of several houses. One house had a life-sized plastic nativity scene brightly lit in the front yard. The Virgin Mary smiled beatifically at Desirée as the other figures stared in joyful admiration of the child in the manger.

No one does Christmas like Texas does Christmas.

Big.

She exited the car and slammed the door shut—both shaking the necklace of dried marigolds hanging from her rearview mirror and startling the figure in the complex's bottom-floor window from his soporific haze. He watched as her black patent leather pumps, which extended out from under a laughably large winter coat that nearly engulfed her body, clicked their way to apartment B. The complex was set up so that each apartment had a door with a direct entrance to the outside. Sort of like a Motel 6. But remarkably dingier.

The nettlesome buzz of the electric doorbell droned from behind the wooden frame. Desirée heard a clicking noise, as if the door were unlocking itself. She tentatively pushed the door open, unsure whether another person would be standing on the other side.

There was no one.

From the doorway, she could see a blue and white tiled bathroom, complete with a curtain-less bathtub, a low sink and a toilet with a metal bar installed in the wall next to it. Down the narrow hallway sat a rarely-used kitchen, which stood in contrast to the Chinese food boxes, plastic forks and empty Coca-Cola cans littering the countertops.

"Matthew?" she called out, hesitant to wade any further into the thick disarray.

"In here," responded a flat voice. She clicked her way towards the voice to what she assumed was the bedroom. The wooden floors creaked as she slowed her gait and shifted her balance towards the room, nearly stepping on a small, fragrant wreath lying in front of the door. An exposed nail suggested the wreath once hung there. She placed the wreath onto the nail, restoring the foyer to its previously festive glory.

The holiday season, however, had not touched Matthew's room, which stood in antithesis to his neighbors' ostentatious yuletide displays. Desirée quickly took in the blank white walls, a full-sized mattress on the floor, a basic "self-assembly" desk with an old MacBook Air on top and three milk crates piled on each other, brimming with papers, books on various computer languages and other office-like odds and ends. The miniature air conditioner, which normally made its year-round home mounted within the window, sat upon a tattered green towel in the corner. An electric space heater hummed next to the A/C. Though it emitted a two-foot radius of heat from its bellowing core, the room remained chilly.

It was one of the most pitiful sights she had ever encountered.

Matthew sat in a chair next to the window. A stained gray blanket covered most of his body. He sat stone-faced in his assessment of her. She kept her hand on the knob, pausing in silence. It lasted only half a second, but Matthew saw the look of startled uncertainty flash across her eyes. He tightened his grip on the gray blanket as she drew a tight smile across her lips and clicked through the archway.

"Matthew?" she asked in her soft Texas drawl.

"Who else would I be?" was his surly reply.

She cleared her throat before continuing, "Of course. I'm Desirée."

He stared at her in the same stony silence that first greeted her. She guessed he was less of the "needs to be warmed up" type and more of the "gets right down to business" sort of fellow.

"You're late," he finally declared, indicating the digital alarm clock sitting on top of the milk crates. 4:27PM glowed in red.

She took a calming breath.

"You're right," she admitted, a crisp edge sneaking into her words. "I am late. And I'm sure you've noticed it's quite cold outside. Frost covering the ground and everything—which made driving on I-69 rather treacherous. There was a bad accident, which had traffic tied up for a few miles. And since I don't have your number, I couldn't call to warn you about my tardiness. I'm normally quite punctual. But don't worry, you'll still get your full hour."

A confused look crossed Matthew's face, but he continued to say nothing as Desirée slid her ponderous coat off her shoulders.

"Is this a good place for it?" she asked delicately, referring to the stack of milk crates.

"It's fine," he cautiously muttered.

She softly placed her coat on top of the pile and then turned her attention towards him.

"So," she cooed seductively, skimming her hands over her hips, "I'm told it's your birthday." The purple silk dress clung to her body, accentuating each inviting curve.

In spite of her obvious allure, Matthew stared disdainfully at her.

Desirée continued the seduction. "Forty-four years old. You could be my father, but then again, I like older men." She shifted her weight to her left side, sticking out her hip and running her flaming red nails over the top of her conspicuous breasts.

"What does Daddy want, hmmm? What would make him feel so good, so special on his special day?" she purred.

As she stepped towards Matthew, he snickered derisively at her.

"Jesus fucking Christ," he said, placing his head in his hand in disbelief.

She halted mid-step.

"What the fuck are you doing, huh? What the hell is wrong with you?" he asked.

She looked at him stunned, not quite believing the unfolding events.

"Are you not understanding me?" he continued. "*No comprendes? No habla ingles*, you trashy whore? You're disgusting. This *act* is disgusting. I can't *fucking* believe Julian set this shit up. 'Package' my ass."

"Package?" Desirée shook her head in confusion.

"If he thought I would enjoy this, the least he could have done was send me someone who wasn't so pathetic!" He spat out the last word like a lethal bullet. Her stony gaze never wavered from his assault, but her fiery look proved his words had their intended effect.

After several moments of heated silence, Desirée finally asked, "Are you finished?"

He paused for a second, but before he could open his mouth to respond, she venomously spat, "Because I think we are quite finished here. You have no consideration for the pains that it's taken me to get here. I've tried to be nice to you, and then you *insult* me for no goddamned reason!"

Desirée escalated her tirade, as Matthew grew steadily more uneasy.

"What the fuck am *I* doing? What the hell is wrong with *me*? What the hell is wrong with *you*? You need to take a good, hard look in the mirror, buddy. You want to talk about pathetic? I'm not the one living in a shithole, smelling like piss and old Chinese food. I'm not the one who needs his friend to set him up so he can get laid. And I'm certainly not the one sitting there like some limp-dick *maricón* with some ratty-ass blanket wrapped around him!"

She grabbed the edge of Matthew's gray comforter and in one, satisfying yank tore it from his body. She regretted the decision even before the wool fringes left her fingertips and fell to the scratched hardwood floor. The sight before her concomitantly halted her breath and flushed her cheeks. Her flames of anger immediately extinguished and compassion crept into her heart.

Matthew sat in an armless wheelchair. The blanket—which had previously surrounded his slumped shoulders—had deftly camouflaged the back of the seat. A newly-revealed colostomy bag hung next to his hips. But what held her attention were his legs: baggy black sweatpants draped over his thighs, hiding them from plain sight, but the bony outline underneath clearly revealed profound emaciation. Scabbed flesh peeked out from the space between where his pants tapered on his shins and where his gray, wool socks sat just above the ankle. His feet twisted limply on the black footplates.

Desirée remained frozen with her mouth agape before gathering her wits.

"I'm so sorry," she pleaded. "I didn't mean to call you what I called you. I was just so angry and, I didn't know. I mean Julian didn't tell me that you were—"

Mortified by her behavior, she was unable to say the words. Hoping to end her embarrassment, she abruptly turned on her heel and made her way towards the exit.

"I didn't know, either!" he cried out to her.

She turned and looked at him with dark eyes that saw the remnants of a man whose world had taught him that he was no more than a forgotten pile of unmovable and unlovable flesh and bone. His entreating words proved that he—like all of her customers—had desires, yearnings and needs. Her professionalism coupled with a deeper calling kept her from walking out the door.

When he saw Desirée's growing compassion, Matthew knew he'd been exposed. His loneliness was now her potential weapon, which caused his tone to shift instantly to nonchalance.

"Julian didn't tell me who you were. He just said a package was being delivered at 4pm today."

As the puzzle clicked together in Desirée's mind, she too put her head in her hand just as Matthew had a few moments ago.

"Jesus fucking Christ," she said.

"Exactly."

"Why would he do that?" she asked, shaking her head in befuddlement.

"Probably because he knew I wouldn't have agreed to this bullshit. No offense."

She said nothing, but he could see his words had offended her.

"Look," he said. "You're paid for, right?"

Despite his ill choice of words, she nodded her assent.

"Why don't you stay for a bit. No expectations. You made the trip up here in the frost and you don't *have* to leave just yet. If you don't want to."

The eyes that saw everything whispered to her skeptical, distrusting mind, and in spite of her better judgment, it was the heart that ultimately spoke on her behalf.

"Do you want me to stay?" she asked, requesting his overt compliance.

"Yes," he replied.

"All right," she said. "But if I stay, we play by my rules."

Matthew hesitated for a moment before conceding.

"Fine," he answered. "What are your rules?"

Despite her overwhelming and immediate sympathy for him, she kept her guard up.

"First of all," she began, "no name-calling. *¿Entiendes?*"

"Yes," he simply replied.

"Second, I am here for one hour and one hour only. I've already been here for seven minutes, so we are down to fifty-three minutes."

He nodded his head.

"Third, you do not touch me without my express consent and likewise, I will not touch you without your permission."

"Yup."

"Fourth, we are going to work *with* each other to make this time together the most pleasant and best use of your money. I need you to communicate clearly with me. Any more fighting or badgering and I'm gone."

"Okay."

"Finally, I am a professional. I expect to be treated like one. Moreover, I am a human being, so a little kindness wouldn't hurt."

After a few seconds, Matthew conceded.

"Fine," he said.

"Good. Now, here's your blanket." She passed the wool comforter back to him, averting her eyes as he quickly covered himself again.

"So may I have something to drink?" she asked.

"Only got water from the tap and Coke in the fridge. No fancy champagne or nothing," he replied, another a twinge of embarrassment coloring his voice.

"Water is just fine," she said, placing her coat back on the milk crates. "I'm driving home after this and the conditions are definitely not suitable for even the mildly inebriated." She allowed herself to slightly smile as she finished her sentence.

Matthew exited the bedroom and wheeled his way towards the kitchen. She listened as he opened and closed the cabinets and heard him rustling out a Solo cup from a plastic sleeve. He turned on the faucet, filling the cup with water.

She stood waiting as the plastic sleeve crinkled once more. Matthew opened the freezer, plunged his hand into the ice tray and removed and dropped four cubes into the cup. She listened to the pop of a can opening, followed by the sound of fizzy soda pouring over crackling ice.

He placed the empty can on the counter along with the rest of his collection and made his way back to the room, skillfully balancing two cups in one hand as he operated the chair with the other.

"Here you are," he said, offering the cup to Desirée like an olive branch.

She stood tall in front of him and raised her drink to the sky.

"Happy Birthday, Matthew McDonald. Here's to new beginnings."

"To new beginnings," he replied, slightly beguiled by her unexpected toast.

She bent down, clicked his cup with a pliant thud and emptied the vessel's contents in one thirsty gulp.

"Man, I needed that," she panted, trying to catch her breath after her marathon guzzle. She glanced around the room for a moment before returning her focus to Matthew and asked, "Do you have another chair?"

"In the bathroom, folded up by the sink."

She remembered seeing the bathroom directly across the hall from the bedroom, so she quickly trotted through the entryway, found the chair and unfolded it in front of Matthew. She sat down with an elegant plop, crossed her legs and placed her hands in her lap. Matthew sat up a bit more, mirroring her poise and attention.

She studied Matthew for a moment before she spoke.

"So, it seems we began on the wrong foot. Let's start this again, shall we?"

Matthew nervously glanced at the clock, and then met her gaze again. His lack of objection was her signal to continue.

"Hi, my name is Desirée. You must be Matthew. Your friend Julian sent me here to help you celebrate your birthday."

"Well, not to be rude or nothing, Miss Desirée, but as good as Julian's intentions may be, I'm not too interested in your kind of celebrating."

Desirée's eyes softened a little as she responded, "We don't have to do anything you don't want to do. Really. I've had clients come to me and all they want is to talk. Some of them just want me to hold them. Others want to watch me undress and touch myself. So, just know, that there isn't any pressure from me for you to do *anything*."

Matthew cast his eyes downward. Desirée kept her focus on him, anticipating a response to emerge from his impassivity. When none arose, she took the initiative.

"So, how do you know Julian?"

He curled his lips in a wry smile and said, "Man, you sure know how to get right to it, don't you?"

She cocked her head to the side and furrowed her brows in confusion.

"Julian was there when *this* happened." He opened his palms and held them downward, indicating his cadaverous lower extremities.

"Oh. Sorry," she said, embarrassment creeping into her voice once more.

"Ah, don't worry about it. Not like it's any big secret. Julian and I were both in Desert Storm together. Army. We were stationed in Saudi Arabia, not far from Kuwait. We were bunkmates. The Scud alarms had been going off every night all week, so I wasn't too concerned when we'd heard them. That night, after dinner, we went back to our room, playing cards, talking about our girlfriends, what we missed about home. All that shit. After a few hours, we got tired and were getting ready for bed. I got up to go take a leak. As I stood up, I saw through my window a missile, only seconds from hitting the barracks. I didn't even think. I just cursed out loud, grabbed Julian and hit the floor. That's all I remember before everything went black."

Matthew snapped his fingers, emphasizing his sudden loss of consciousness. Desirée watched with compassion and curiosity.

"The next thing I know I'm at the medical center. My body covered in bandages. My chest in agonizing pain. Turns out I had five broken ribs, a punctured lung and shrapnel all in my legs and back. One piece sliced right through my T-9 vertebra."

Desirée winced at the detailed description of his injury.

"Yeah, well, as painful as that sounds, it's nothing compared to the shit you have to deal with afterwards. The rehab. Watching your muscles atrophy. Bedsores. Spasming. Infections. To this day I still wonder if everything would've been better if I'd just died that night."

She stared in pained silence as Matthew's morbid daydream sank in.

"Julian credits me for saving him," he continued, oblivious to the effect his previous words had on her. "And, I don't know, maybe even blames himself a little for my condition. In any case, he's been a good friend—my only friend, really—since that night."

Matthew tossed his head to the side, indicating the front door.

"He's the one that brought over the wreath, which I noticed you put back in place."

Desirée smiled, appreciating that her care did not go unnoticed.

"He seems like a good friend to you," she remarked. "Though it's still odd that Julian would enroll my services as part of your birthday present without telling you."

"Yeah, that's Julian. He has a good heart, but his common sense leaves a lot to be desired."

"True," she said, grinning conspiratorially. "Are you originally from Harlingen? I don't hear an accent."

"No, Harrisburg."

"Pennsylvania?"

"Yup. Ever been there?"

"No. I just know it's the capital."

"Yeah, well, you're not missing much," he said with contempt. "Amish and Hershey's and cold-ass winters. That's about it. Being the only black kid in school made for one hell of an education."

"How?" she inquired.

"Well, you learn pretty quickly what it means to be different. I didn't have to remember what color my skin was. People took it upon themselves to remind me every damn day—whether I wanted them to or not."

"I see," said Desirée knowingly. Matthew looked down at his hands, picking at his fingernails.

"So what brought you here?" asked Desirée, hoping to bring his attention back to the conversation.

"A woman," he replied. "Well, two women, really."

Desirée raised her eyebrows at his humorously salacious response.

He laughed.

"Yeah, it's not what you think. After the war, Julian was living in Carlisle while his girlfriend, now wife, was finishing school. He would drive over a lot and check in on me. My girlfriend at the time, Sara, wasn't handling my condition so well. Probably because *I* wasn't handling my condition so well. We'd always had this 'on-again/off-again' kind of relationship. Anyway, Julian's girlfriend was all freaked out after what happened in the Gulf. She wanted to get married and have kids. Get that family going before something awful happened to him. They moved here so she could be closer to her parents. Sara finally left me soon after, so Julian invited me to stay with him while I continued my recovery. So I guess you could say one woman drove me out of Pennsylvania and another one dragged me here."

Matthew paused, taking in the woman who sat attentively and patiently before him. The stillness and poise with which she held herself was something he'd rarely seen. It fascinated and unnerved him.

"You're an interesting one," he finally remarked.

"Why's that?" she asked, curious of his assessment of her.

"I mean, we weren't exactly best buds when you first walked in here, and now you've got me yapping away. I've told more to you in twenty-five minutes than I've told other people in twenty-five years."

"Does that bother you?"

"No, it's just interesting. Why don't you tell me about yourself? Let me guess: whore-by-day, whore-by-night, huh?"

"What?!" she exclaimed, offended by his coarse assessment.

"No, no—I didn't mean it in a bad way. I just mean, well, I can't see someone like you working at Wal-Mart and going to knitting circles. So I'm guessing that you don't do much more than this."

"There is much more to me than *this*," she declared, the steely defensiveness returning to her eyes.

"Look, forget it Desirée. I'm sorry. It was a dumb comment. Just tell me something about yourself." His contrite expression mollified the rage within her. When she stepped back from the coarseness of his words, she saw that he was a man clumsily trying to make her laugh. It was kind of sweet.

"Well," she began, testing the edges of her own retracting anger, "what do you want to know?"

"Why don't we start with 'Where are you from?'"

"Brownsville."

"And your parents?"

She tightened her lips before responding in a clipped tone, "My mother's from Mexico."

"Ah. And your father?"

She paused, unsure whether or not she wanted to continue.

"Born in Dallas."

"How did you end up in Brownsville?" asked Matthew.

"I was born there. My father moved to Cameron County in the late '80s. That's where he met my mother. She had dreamed of living in the United States and had a cousin there. My mom knew she wanted children someday and wanted to give them 'The American Dream.' Freedom. Opportunity. All that stuff you see in the movies. I was her impetus to cross the border. So she spent her entire life savings on a *coyote* and walked for four days through the Sonoran desert. Not many people can survive a trip like that. She credits *la Virgen de Guadalupe* with keeping her alive. Every morning, to this day, she picks up her rosary, lights a candle and says a prayer of gratitude to Mother Mary. Faith—that is a woman who embodies faith."

She glanced at the smiling figure of Mary, gleaming from across the street.

"This is her favorite time of year," she continued. "She sees it as a time when all of humanity's faith in Jesus is restored."

"And your mother named you Desirée? Seems like an odd choice for such a pious woman."

"I call myself Desirée, but that's not the name she gave me."

"What's your real name?"

"That, Mr. McDonald, is a trade secret. Discretion is at the heart of what I do—and that discretion works both ways," she replied, a slight smirk spreading across her painted, red lips.

"Understandable."

A weighted silence descended over them as they sat, unsure of where to move the conversation. Finally, Matthew's boldness caught up with his curiosity.

"Can I ask you something kind of personal?" he blurted out.

"You may *ask*, but that's no guarantee I'll *answer*."

He chuckled at her coy response.

"Fair enough. I guess I just want to know how does someone end up doing this kind of work?"

"It wasn't that difficult a decision to make. A girl I knew from college did it to pay for school. She introduced me to the right people. One night I gave it a try. It wasn't as hard as I initially thought it would be. The guy was harmless—sweet even. Really wanted to make sure I was just as satisfied as he was. But what really got me was the money. I'd made more in two hours than my mother made in a week."

"Wow."

"Yeah. I finally saw my way out."

"Out of what?" he asked.

"Out of this shitty-ass life. Out of watching my mother slave for twelve hours a day. Out of feeling powerless against the hand I was dealt. As much as I was *dying* to leave town to go to an ivy-league school, I couldn't leave my mother behind. With this job, I could go anywhere I wanted and take her with me."

"What about your father?"

She could feel the tears swell even before he finished the question.

"Papa died when I was ten. He was a social worker. Got shot coming home one day. Wrong place, wrong time."

"Oh my God. I'm so sorry."

"It's-it's OK," she said, trying to brush it off. "It was thirteen years ago."

"Wait. How old are you?" Matthew asked, the math calculating in his scrambling head.

"Twenty-three."

"*Fuck me!*" he cried. "Jesus, you're just a girl. I thought you were at least thirty or something!"

"Yeah, well, when you start accompanying fifty-year-old men to fundraisers and banquet dinners, they put a lot of money into making sure you look mature and respectable."

"I guess," he replied, still shaking his head in amazement.

"Look," Desirée said, hoping to clarify the situation, "I'm paying my way through law school. I'm not here for the so-called 'glamour.' It's not all rich guys and jewels and *Pretty Woman* romance. It's work. Some days it's not so great, but most of the time it's fine. I show up. I do my thing. I go home. And I've been doing it long enough now that I get to choose my clients. Where, when, how—you name it. And that's saying a lot for a woman in *any* profession. I only took this gig—"

She stopped mid-sentence, taking in the squalor of Matthew's surroundings. Not wanting to shame him any more than she already had, she changed tactics.

"Julian knows some good people and has been very generous to me. So when he set up this little birthday gift for you, it was my pleasure to aid and abet him."

"And you know Julian how?"

Desirée paused, carefully considering her words before simply repeating, "Julian knows some good people."

Matthew sighed.

"Not to be offensive or nothing, but don't you care that he has a wife?" he asked.

"I don't ask too many questions," she answered. "That's why clients like me. It builds trust. I don't push my nose in their business. They get enough of that from everyone else."

"Hmph," Matthew replied, somewhat unconvinced.

"I got you talking pretty quick, didn't I?" she said teasingly.

Matthew couldn't help but grin, realizing that, once again, she had him caught.

"You have a nice smile," she remarked with genuine affection.

Matthew's momentary liveliness sank once again into melancholy.

"Not much to smile about," he said.

"Well, if I may be blunt here, that's nobody's fault but your own," she responded.

"I thought you said you didn't push your nose into other people's business," he remarked, his eyes narrowing into scrutinizing slits.

"I've been known to improvise," she replied.

Matthew laughed again, softening at her playful repartee.

After his chuckling had died down, she decided to test the boundary of the conversation once more.

"But seriously, Matthew, all kidding aside, I do see a man who is not giving himself a chance. When I walked in today, you felt like a stone wall. There was no opportunity for me to reach you. No opening for connection. You can't live your life always ready for battle—that's what my mother always says. You must fight when life demands that from you, but you must also know when to lay down the armor."

"This is the only way I know how to survive," he said, all humor gone from his voice.

"Oh! Okay. So you *do* want to live," she pointedly declared, as if catching him with his hand in the cookie jar.

"Huh?"

"Well, earlier you'd talked about how you wondered whether or not your life should have ended the day you got injured. But you are a survivor. You continue to *choose* survival."

He rubbed the heels of his hands in his eyes in exasperation.

"I don't know, girl. I'm just trying to get by, just like you and just like most everyone else on this planet. And I got it pretty good: a job where I can work from home, the VA clinic ten minutes away, a fair amount of my sanity and at least one decent person who gives a shit about me."

"So what's stopping you?"

"Huh?"

"You said you've got it pretty good. What's stopping you from being happy?"

"Jesus, if I knew this was going to turn into an inquisition I would've let you walk out that door."

"Then why did you ask me to stay?" Desirée asked.

"I don't know. I guess I didn't want you to think I was an asshole," he responded.

"What else?"

"And—you seemed nice."

"And?"

"It gave me hope."

"Hope for what?"

He stared at her, unable to answer her question.

"I'm not trying to pressure you," she said, her conciliatory tone doing little to assuage his agitation. "I'm simply trying to understand you."

"What's there to understand?" he retorted. "I'm just a lonely, fucked-up man with a limp dick—just like you said."

"Geez, Matthew. How do you deal with it?" she asked unfazed, shaking her head in wonder.

"With what?"

"The self-hatred. Clearly not with women like me, so what keeps you going? Alcohol? Gambling? Marijuana?"

"None of those things," he replied. "That's the easy way out. There is nothing more punishing than the stone-cold loneliness of sobriety."

"Soldier of pain, huh?" she said, an ironic smile curling on the left side of her mouth.

"Not really," he answered. "It's just that half of me is already numbed out. Might as well try to feel something with what's left."

She took a breath as his last statement sunk in. Feel. He wanted to *feel* something.

"When was the last time you—?" she trailed off, gesticulating towards the lower portion of his body.

"What? Fucked?"

"To put it crudely, yes."

"Don't remember," he said. "Maybe Sara? No, wait."

He stopped suddenly as the dormant past awoke before his eyes.

"There was this one woman, Phuong. Lived in San Jose. Sara and I were 'off-again' at the time. I'd finished my training at Fort Irwin and had a few days free before heading to the Gulf. Huh, funny. I'd forgotten about her until now."

Matthew's eyes wandered out the window as the once-distant memory came into focus.

"Are you afraid?" Desirée asked, snapping Matthew back to the present.

"Of getting rejected? Shit, I gave up on women years ago."

"No," she clarified. "Of feeling something?"

He froze, blindsided by her comment.

She gingerly continued, "Maybe afraid of feeling something in a place where you had given up hope? Maybe hope is the real terror here and self-hatred is the crutch?"

He swallowed, a dry lump forming in his throat.

She paused, surprised at her strange investment in Matthew's personal life. She was never this bold when speaking with her regular clients. Honest, sure. But something about seeing this man on the edge of some sort of realization kept her pushing him further than she normally would.

Beams from the descending sun crossed her face. The neighbor's nativity scene lit up as a tinny version of "Silent Night" began to play.

Wiping the sweat from his forehead, Matthew glanced at the clock, hoping time would be his savior.

"Aren't we almost finished?" he asked, desperate to truncate her examination. "What was it, rule number three?"

"Two," she corrected. "And I said 'one hour and one hour only.' No more—and no less. We still have twenty-one minutes."

The two stared at each other in a breathless stalemate—neither one daring to move, lest the other break the tenuous thread keeping them together.

Finally, on the softest of exhales, Matthew whispered, "Fine."

She raised her eyebrows, surprised at his invitation.

"What do you want, Matthew?" she inquired softly.

"Fine," he repeated. "If you want—if you think you can help me *feel*, then fine."

She placed her hands on her thighs and took a deep breath.

"I've never been with anyone like you before," she warned, as much for herself as for him. "I can't make any promises or guarantees. I just believe, at the risk of sounding trite, that everyone deserves a chance and you never know until you try."

"I'm clean," he blurted out, clipping off the end of her sentence.

"What?" she said, trying to hold back her amusement.

"Not in an STD way—I mean *yes*! In an STD way, too. But I mean, I cleaned myself—with soap—before you came over here. Julian required it. I didn't understand it at the time. Now I know why."

Matthew snickered at Julian's scheme.

"Good to know," she said, feeling like a true gift to Matthew for the first time since entering. "So, what's the first step?"

"You tell me."

"Well, how do we get your pants off?"

"That's not too difficult," he said, untying the white string on his sweatpants. "I just gotta lean to the side and you can shimmy them off."

"Okay." She walked over to him and kneeled down. Meeting his eyes, she asked, "May I touch you?"

He stopped his movements, surprised at her question.

"Hmmm."

"What?" she inquired.

"Nothing—it's just that—well, no one's ever asked that kind of permission before."

"Oh, well, that's just the way it's done. That way everyone's happy."

"No, no, it makes sense. It's just new to me."

"Ah. So, may I touch you?"

"Yes!" he exclaimed, realizing he hadn't answered her initial question.

She gripped his waistband, steadied her gaze and began to gently slide his pants down, careful to avoid the catheter tubing attached to his lower abdomen. When the pants reached his ankles, she pulled off his socks one at a time, then removed the bunched up black fabric of his sweatpants over his naked feet. She surveyed his bare legs. Thin. Very thin. And mottled. Sagging. Ashen—as if a thick, white paste were sloppily smeared over his skin. She softly placed her hands on his shins, feeling the coolness of his legs. She slid her palms over his knees and thighs, stopping at the edge of his groin.

Realizing he was now completely exposed, Matthew quickly looked directly at her.

"Nothing left to hide," he said, shrugging his shoulders. The brittle, forced humor in his tone could not conceal his nervous fragility.

His flaccid cock sat innocently upon his lap upon a backdrop of coarse, black hair. Desirée smelled an acrid mix of musk, salt, baby powder and Irish Spring.

"Ummm, I have to admit," she tentatively began, "I'm not sure what to do."

"That makes two of us," he replied.

She laughed.

"I'm just going to go slow and you tell me to stop anytime. Okay?"

He nodded, eyes never leaving her.

She brought her left hand underneath him, cradling his cock and balls, and placed her right hand on top, creating an egg-shaped cocoon with her fingers. He was surprisingly warm. A low hum vibrated against her palms. She couldn't tell if it came from him or her. She leaned her head down, slightly opened her palms and kissed the tip of his cock.

Matthew inhaled sharply. Though he kept his focus on Desirée, his body remained stiff. She sensed his unease and paused to look at him. The warm acceptance in her eyes eased some of his discomfort. When she felt him settle a bit, she parted her wet lips and slipped them over the head of his cock. Her tongue gently lapped against him. She held him here, melting the slick walls of her cheeks into him. She felt him, malleable and tender—nothing like the armored, military fighter she'd met just under an hour ago.

Desirée began to suck. Despite Matthew's obvious flaccidity, she felt a subtle responsiveness—a pulsing tingle in the back of her throat. She drew him in closer to her. Desirée's desire to bring him in deeper thawed his reticence. Matthew silently yielded to her inviting mouth. She continued to suck, her mouth dripping with saliva. The tingle continued to grow. Burning heat expanded over her neck, face and chest, traveling down until it hit right in the center of her own pussy.

A low grunt freed itself from Matthew's constricted throat. Strange. Though he couldn't feel her mouth on him directly, he was keenly aware of a galvanic shiver creeping over his skin. His breath hitched. Unsure of what was happening, he stiffened his torso.

Desirée sensed his retraction and slowed down. She turned her gaze upwards and saw Matthew staring at her, tension locked in his eyes.

"I-I'm scared," he whispered.

Without thinking, she freed her right hand, which had been steadying the base of his cock, and slid it underneath his sweatshirt, resting it on his bare chest.

Matthew couldn't contain himself anymore. Her attention, her kindness—it was his undoing. Hot, thick tears skimmed down his cheeks and dripped onto his shirt, dampening the back of Desirée's hand. They remained in complete stillness as a wide, crackling force pulsed through them: eyes, tears, heart, hand, mouth, cock, throat, pussy—all creating a pathway for the magnetic current drawing them together.

The white, blistering electricity rumbled through them, timelessly holding them captive. Finally, as the dam began to crack, Matthew spoke.

"I'm sorry," he said brokenly, his swollen throat choking his words. "I'm so sorry." He kept repeating his apology, again and again, his body quaking with sorrow.

As her caretaking instincts took over, she gently removed her mouth from his formless cock and stood up, skimming her body against his until her breasts landed perfectly in line with his heart. She pulled him towards her, wrapping her arms around his torso and cradling the back of his head with her right hand.

"Yes, yes, yes," she said, over and over, as the flood of grief arose and washed over him, carrying her along with the wave. Matthew's pyretic skin blazed, igniting her own inner fire and through this searing union, she felt his agony, loneliness, disappointment and despair. But instead of stonewalling the emotions like she usually did, she allowed them to penetrate her and burn clean in the embers of her fiery heart. A deep understanding of her place in the world filled her with each scorching breath. Finally after several minutes, Matthew's sobs subsided and cool tranquility settled into both of their bodies.

When the storm had passed, she took his face in her hands and softy kissed each of his eyelids. He sat, immobilized and dazed.

"In all the years of my life, even the years when I was walking, I've never felt anything like that," he said, astonishment and gratitude swelling in his eyes.

Desirée silently located the discarded blanket underneath the desk and covered his legs. She then dug around in her purse and procured two square packets. She delicately clicked her way to the kitchen, found a saucepan in a cabinet of forgotten cookware and began boiling water.

Four minutes later she returned with two paper cups of tea and a handful of paper napkins. She placed the tea on the desk and sat down in her chair, still holding the napkins. For several minutes she kept her attention on him as he sat absorbed in thought.

Eventually, Matthew lifted his glassy eyes to hers, pointed to the napkins and asked, "May I have one of those?"

"Of course," she answered, leaning forward to hand him the pile. He mopped up his cheeks before giving his nose a good blow. He quickly grabbed another one and blew again.

"Sorry," he said, laughing as the snot dribbled down his hands.

"No problem," she replied, laughing with him.

When he finished cleaning his face, he looked over at the cups on the desk.

"For me?" he asked. She nodded. "Where'd ya get the tea from?"

"I brought some of my own. I always keep a fresh stock of supplies. Though I didn't think to bring my own dishware, so I just rinsed out these old Starbucks cups I found on your counter and *voilà*! Good as new."

He smiled at her ingenuity as he reached for the tea. He blew off the steam to cool the liquid before taking a sip.

"It's chamomile," she explained, answering his unspoken question. "Good for calming the nerves."

"Thank you," he said.

They sat in silence for a few minutes, re-collecting themselves after the intensity of their encounter.

Matthew broached the subject first.

"Have you ever, um, does that happen often with your—er—clients?"

She shook her head. "No, Matthew. That was a first."

"Oh."

"How are you feeling?"

"Honestly," he replied, "I have no fuckin' clue. I just feel—I don't know—mixed up. Crazy."

"Raw?"

"Yes. Raw. Definitely raw."

"Yeah."

"And grateful."

She looked at him, surprised and touched by his bold tenderness.

He continued, "I'm not clear on what this is or what it means for me or for us. Hell, I don't even know if I'll ever see you again. But I do know something has opened in me. Some feeling of possibility."

She leaned forward, enveloped his hand in hers and looked him dead in the eye.

"You're a good man, Matthew McDonald, who deserves to be loved. No matter what happened in the past—the war, Sara, whatever—don't ever forget that you are worthy of love."

He squeezed her hand, taking in the sincerity of her words.

Though she couldn't quite articulate it in that moment, something opened for her as well. Some power. Some strength. Some capacity for love she'd never known. It softened and confused her. The staunch clarity she'd had when she drove up to his place just over an hour ago had been replaced with the uncertain colors of a turning kaleidoscope. The early sunset streamed through the windows, warming the panes and melting the frost into ribbons of water.

She pulled her hand away from Matthew and placed the cup on the desk.

"Time to go?" he asked tentatively, not quite ready to face the loneliness once more.

"I think so, Matthew," she said, putting on her coat. "But perhaps I could stop by again sometime when I'm in the neighborhood and we could have another cup of tea."

"I'd like that," he replied, warming at the prospect of a new friend.

"Happy Birthday."

"Thank you. And Merry Christmas to you."

"To you as well."

She began to circle towards the door, then paused as the soft edges of the kaleidoscope came into perspective.

"Magdalena," she said, her back still to him.

"Excuse me?" he asked.

She turned to face him. "Magdalena. It's the name my mother gave me. It was her hometown."

"Oh," he said, surprised at her unforeseen act of intimacy.

"I figure if we're going to be friends, we might as well start out knowing each other's names."

"Of course," he replied, touched by her generosity. "And I'm sorry."

She gave him a puzzled look.

"If we're going to be friends, then I'd like to apologize. I'm sorry that I called you all those things when we first met."

She smiled warmly. "Accepted."

"And you're right," he continued, awe and gratitude in his voice. "You are so much more than *this*."

His words rung inside her for moment and echoed through the shifting kaleidoscope before finally locking it into place.

"No," she declared. "I *am* this. And there is nothing more I need to be." She clicked past the door in her black heels—stopping momentarily to admire the handmade wreath once more. Getting in her blue Honda, she briefly paused to run her fingers over the necklace of dried marigolds before starting the car and making her way home—the crisp, Texan sunset riding shotgun.

the warrior archetype
TRUTH, AGENCY

> *Most maidens are perfectly capable of rescuing themselves in my experience, at least the ones worth something, in any case.* ~ Erin Morgenstern, The Night Circus

The Warrior archetype is often associated with men and hyper-masculinity. However, history has many examples of warrior women; indeed, their essence lives in the collective feminine psyche today. The Warrior is the one who defends freedom and fights for justice at all costs. She's like the honey badger from the viral YouTube video: she takes what she wants and doesn't give a shit—as long as it is in service to liberation.

Her erotic nature is of pure presence and penetration. She is always on alert and uses unrelenting strength of will and spirit to cut through the bullshit and touch the truth of any moment. Whereas many archetypes use their erotic energy for uninhibited creation, the Warrior is the editor, destroying all that is false or redundant and crafting her expression so others may receive its purest distillation.

In the sexual realm, the Warrior wastes no time entertaining resistance and with her laser focus, she cuts through emotional bondage—freeing desire. She is the one who proclaims that she's going to "fuck your brains out," "tear your ass in two," and "fucking devour you"—always in service to the highest good, of course.

The Warrior is one of the most potent forces for awakening. With the popularity of yoga in Western culture over the past hundred years, the Hindu goddess Kali Ma—with her bloody scimitar, necklace of skulls, and long, wagging tongue—is one of the more recognizable images of the feminine Warrior.

Kali also invokes the spirit of the Mother along with the Warrior. We can see this Mother/Warrior blend in our society in women who fiercely defend their families. Even women who don't have biological children can still embody the Mother/Warrior aspect—think of social workers, lawyers, and activists who devote their lives to women's and children's rights. They are the protectors of the innocent.

The term "spiritual warrior" is now popular due to the New Age spiritual movement. This means to become a defender of our own truth and a slayer of the egoic patterns that hold us back from full self-expression.

The feminine spiritual warrior learns how to rise up above the "fairy tale promise" of "the one" saving her from the "locked tower." Instead, she discovers that in reality the keys to her freedom lie in her own hands. Only when she is willing to sacrifice the scripted "fairy tale ending" and become her own hero does she discover her power. From this place, she can then embrace the masculine from wholeness, rather than needing him for her completion.

The term "warrior" came into English from the Old Northern French word *werreier*—a variant of the Old French *guerroieor* or "one who wages war." The word "war" comes from the Old High German word meaning "to confuse." Often when the Warrior archetype emerges, she throws our whole world into confusion. Everything we thought we were gets stripped away, and we are frequently left with the confounding question, "Who am I?" If we surrender to the Warrior's wisdom, that answer often rings clearer with each slice of her sharp blade.

the shadow warrior

The Warrior has several shadows, namely the Murderer, the Avenger, the Judge, and the Masochist. If the Warrior has no connection to any morals and simply kills on every impulse, she is an incarnation of the Murderer. Serial killers and mercenaries are the prime example of this shadow. If her destructive power is linked to a personal injustice, then she is the Avenger, using her power based on *her* interpretation of what is true and just. Images of Clint Eastwood from *The Man with No Name* trilogy or Uma Thurman as The Bride from *Kill Bill* come to mind.

If the Warrior is connected to an unwavering sense of moral rectitude, then we have the Judge who metes out justice based on a belief that a certain dogma is the most correct truth. Prime examples of these are Judge Danforth from Arthur Miller's *The Crucible*, certain fascist military commanders, and many modern-day, fanatical religious leaders. Finally, if the destruction is turned inward and is linked with a lack of personal value and self-esteem, we see the Masochist, unable to move forward and constantly berating herself for her imperfection. The Masochist will withstand (and often enmesh her identity with) any amount of pain or torture if it is "for the good of the cause," be that cause for a country, a relationship, or spiritual development.

integrated and shadow examples of the warrior

- Amazons: Race of women warriors from Greek mythology.
- Brünnhilde: Norse/Germanic shieldmaiden and Valkyrie.
- Diana: Roman goddess of the hunt and protector/defender of nature.
- Durga: Hindu warrior goddess and demon slayer who restores justice and peace.
- Harriet Tubman: African-American abolitionist who fought against the injustice of slavery and brought many of her people to freedom.
- Joan of Arc: French military leader who led the charge against the British in the Hundred Years War.
- Maat: Egyptian goddess of integrity, fairness, and justice.
- N'Nonmiton: Real-life warrior women from the

Kingdom of Dahomey, now near present day Benin. Called the Dahomey Amazons by Western observers.
- Onna-bugeisha: Female warriors belonging to noble classes in feudal Japan.
- Wonder Woman: DC Comic Superhero who is an Amazonian Princess and trained warrior—using her golden lasso to mete out justice. Amongst civilians, she is known as Diana Prince.
- Alex Forrest: Glenn Close's character in *Fatal Attraction* (Avenger/Murderer Shadow).
- The Bride from *Kill Bill* (Avenger Shadow).
- Cutters: People who deliberately hurt themselves through cutting their skin (Masochist Shadow).
- Dolores Umbridge: Cruel teacher from the *Harry Potter* book series (Judge Shadow).

inviting the warrior into our lives

It is said that the truth is the biggest turn-on. But in order to get to the truth, we must cut through the protective lies we have built around ourselves. There is a practice called "running withholds" where one person tells the other all the truths that they have been withholding in an effort to reestablish connection within the relationship. Although complicated feelings can and do arise often, the point is not to hurt one another but to simply clear the lenses of perception so partners can see each other clearly. It's about fostering intimacy, not retribution. And the practice of running withholds usually increases the sexual spark more than any position, technique, or pill-based aphrodisiac.

Connect to the potency and strength of the integrated Warrior. She is here to help us move into what we most fear and to guide us on the path to liberation. That may mean giving up the old ways of relating and our expectations of how we think our lives should be. We may feel confused or scared or victimized. That's okay. Be bold—her truth outshines and outlasts any beautiful falsehood we could create for ourselves.

legend of the south seas

My heart hums in a secret volcano
Hidden patiently dormant
Midway between Helena and Espiritu Santo
Teetering on the tip of tectonic bliss

A loner by nature
(She never fit in with Pangea)
She calls the ring of fire
Home

Enigmatic magma rumbles
Beneath her crest
Luring worthy sailors
To slip onto her shores

Map-less, they must brave her currents
(No easy sextant for celestial navigation)
Caressing her whispering zephyrs
Riding her blistering squalls

'Til they wash up famished
On her full, wet sands
Igniting her belly ablaze
Swollen earth morphs to enveloping lava

And in unrivaled eruptions
(Pele is so jealous!)

Impassioned ashes descend
Searing skin-to-skin, soul-to-soul

Immortalizing their bodies
In cinder-splendor
A pacific monument
To her tempestuous love

diana

4am.

A thick July sweat wrapped around Diana as she stood on the side of the road under a flickering streetlamp—the only streetlamp on Salina's far northern drag. American flags celebrating the nation's independence hung limply like overripe fruit in the stagnant air. The humidity, while oppressive, hinted that relief might be in sight from the six-month drought plaguing the town—though it amplified the aches pulsing through Diana's body. Her feet hurt. Her lower back clenched. And the cut on her neck hummed dully throughout her body. The faint smell of blood and beer still clung to her after an excruciating night behind the bar. Attempting to organize the hazy scramble of her thoughts, she silently recounted the past three hours.

Gary, a Saturday usual, had stopped by for his fix. Loud. Crude. Angry. A classic drunkard—down to the rubicund nose that even Bardolph would have mocked. He preferred cheap beer straight from the bottle. Diana knew he had reached his limit three drinks before the incident, but her habit of pocketing any wet, folded dollar bills placed on the padauk counter overrode her inclination to cut him off. Plus, beyond a belligerent rant or two, he'd never gotten violent—and certainly nothing like that night.

His wife was cheating on him—or so he believed? She couldn't remember the details. The customers' orders and replay of the Chiefs game had occupied the bulk of her attention. Gary never talked about his wife, except to complain about how she rarely put out and when she did, "It was like fucking a cold, dead fish."

"Who could blame her?" Diana thought, imagining Gary slamming like a reckless jackhammer into his wife's body. "I'd probably be just as cold and dead as she is—shutting down every bit of feeling just to survive the experience."

However, at the point when he started accusing everyone at the bar of sleeping with his wife, Diana knew it was time to intercede.

"Gary," she told him, "It's time for you to get a cab."

"I don't take orders from you, you fucking fat bitch," he slurred.

She'd worked at The Road Warrior for so long (what was it—fifteen years now, since right after high school?) that she'd learned not to take it personally. For every snide remark about her weight, there were three times the number of sexual propositions. Men either wanted to fuck her or kill her—the common response to a woman in the powerful position of gatekeeper to serving the eternally thirsty.

"Gary, c'mon man," she coaxed. "You're drunk. I'm going to call you cab, and you're going to go home and sleep it off."

"Home?!" he cried. "Home? There is no home. There is no bed. There is no sleeping next to that—that—" His voice strangled a bit as he collapsed onto the bar. Jim, another regular who spent his money slowly nursing Rusty Nails, caught Gary in his hirsute arms and tried to help him stand back up. Gary's wounded pride must have hit its limit in that moment, because he suddenly roared back to life, grabbed Jim's glass and hurled it across the room, screaming, "I don't need your help, motherfucker!"

"Gary!" Diana cried. Without thinking and quite foolishly, she reached out to restrain his monstrous limbs. His angry fingers wrapped around the empty longneck he'd just finished. A scream like nothing she'd ever heard emanated from within him as he swung the bottle at her head. She ducked, barely escaping the improvised weapon, but in his drunkenness, he didn't have a very solid grip on the bottle. Diana turned in time to see the bottle slip from his hand and smash into the glowing display of alcohol behind her. Glass shattered everywhere. Liquor rushed down the damp, dusty wood. Squeezing her eyes shut, she covered her head, but not before a shard of broken bottle ricocheted off the back wall and sliced her neck.

"FUCK!" The stabbing pain nearly knocked her to the ground as she lumbered to the end of the bar, hoping to avoid collapsing on a pile of broken glass. Her hand instinctively found its way to the side of her neck. Blood, more than one typically wants to see coming from one's own body, streamed between the webbing of her fingers. Instinctively, she grabbed a clean-ish towel from the pile next to the sink and quickly ran her finger along the line of sliced skin. Determining that no glass had lodged into her neck, she plunged the towel against the wound and began instructing the men.

"Get him on the ground!" she ordered, her tone mirroring the authoritarian resonance of her military father. Though he died in an ambush in Saudi Arabia when Diana was only eight years old, his unquestionable command left a lasting imprint as she matured.

Her impatience grew as she watched the patrons play an inebriated tug-of-war with Gary's limbs. With one hand nursing her neck, she hopped over the bar—landing behind Gary—and wrapped her free arm around his waist as she kneed the back of his leg. Losing his center of balance, Gary's knee buckled, and he collapsed to the ground. The patrons swirled around him, pinning his limbs to the sticky wood floor.

Amongst the drunken chaos, five or six men managed to hold Gary down long enough for him to surrender. He lay on the ground, his demons exposed, weeping and mumbling, "She's dead, she's dead," mourning a ghost from long ago.

Gary's voice trailed off into silence. The men released their grip on him and stepped back. Diana crouched down, checking to see if he was finally comatose. Catching her figure out of the corner of his eye, Gary gripped her hand and furtively whispered as if channeling some supernatural creature, "You—like her—are just a guest house. You too will die. Don't let it be in this place." And with those incoherent parting words, Gary fell totally limp.

Startled at Gary's out-of-character moment of inebriated divination, Diana briefly wondered who "she" was—and were it not for the throbbing pain in her neck or the fact that the alcohol had obliterated Gary's consciousness, she might have inquired further. She looked around to see if anyone else had caught Gary's strange prophecy, but everyone seemed occupied with returning to his own drink and sorrow. Comfort and habit sunk back in as immediately as it had been disrupted.

The manager, who'd been doing inventory in the basement, stepped up from the wooden hatch door and surveyed the destruction before him.

"Out! Everyone out now," he barked. He went by the simple moniker, JB. No last name. Late 60's-ish. Maybe. Worked there for as long as she could remember. Built like a brick, he didn't say much, but when he did, people listened. She liked that about him. His gruff directness. It put her at ease.

It was close to 2am. Most of the customers had already paid their bills and those that hadn't threw some wadded-up cash onto the bar as they rushed out into the warm night—no doubt a relief compared to the thick, acrid stench inside. Jim shook Gary to rustle him awake before aiding him to his feet. Gary half mumbled apologies as Jim carried him towards the door.

"I'll take him home with me," Jim said before the door closed behind them.

Once the place cleared, Diana regained awareness of her frozen state. Except for the aching gash on her neck, she had lost all sensation from the rest of her body. Standing in the heavy silence, she inhaled—her limbs melting a little as warmth returned to her feet and hips. Exhaling, her eyes glazed over as exhaustion rolled through her. A bit woozy, she gripped the Chicago bar rail trying to maintain her balance.

"You ok?" JB inquired. He wasn't concerned with her health or wellbeing but was interested in making sure he didn't have to take care of her. He'd always been uncomfortable when dealing with "feeling" matters. A practical man. Intimacy was not something he did well.

"I'll be ok," she said, wanting his concern as little as he wanted to give it.

"Well, take a few minutes and then we'll clean up."

He handed Diana a glass of water, which she imbibed in one slippery gulp, soothing her scorched throat. As she slid onto a barstool, she stared absently at the wreckage littering the spot where she had stood just ten minutes earlier. JB headed to the back supply room and returned with a dustpan, broom and metal garbage bin. He began sweeping and throwing away mounds of glass in crashing piles.

"I'll help you in a moment. Just gonna check on this," Diana said, indicating her neck. JB kept cleaning—his silence acknowledging that he'd heard her. She placed the glass on the bar and walked to the bathroom. Despite the circles under her eyes and the glassy stare, everything looked ok. The cut had mostly clotted.

Noticing that the wound itself was relatively superficial, she was glad to discover that it had felt a lot worse than it looked. She ran some water over a wad of disposable brown paper towels and gently washed her neck. A cool, sharp sting coursed through her with each dab of the towels. After a few rounds of this, she ambled back to the bar to help JB.

Two hours later, they were finally locking up.

"We'll take care of inventory tomorrow—er, um, later today," JB instructed. "Just get some sleep and be back here at

4:30. If you need the day off, I understand, but I could really use your help."

"I'll be here," she responded automatically, without pausing to make a real decision in the matter.

"Good. Well then, see you later." He made his way to his truck. "Hey, uh—you want a ride?" he asked, as he turned to look at her.

"No thanks," she answered back, a little shocked at his gesture of goodwill. "I'm fine. I'll take the blue route," she lied, knowing full well that the bus didn't run that early—and certainly not on the Lord's Day.

Without a word, he opened the door of his red Chevrolet, got in and drove off.

Diana's surprise at JB's offer was bested only by her decision to decline it. After all the drama of the evening, a ride home *would* have been nice. But something in her needed the clean air, the solitude, the quiet. Besides, despite her exhaustion she was too adrenalized to go straight to bed.

"A walk will do me good," she thought to herself. She jogged across the road, but instead of heading home, she slowed her gait and leaned against the pole with the flickering light.

"What a fucking night," she said aloud.

Her mind returned to Gary and his strange words.

"You—like her—are just a guest house. You too will die. Don't let it be in this place."

She considered the meaning of his ominous forecast for a moment before writing it off as a delusional outburst from a man who'd just been—at least in his mind—cuckolded.

How long had he been married? 15? 20 years? Admittedly, she didn't know the whole story, but if his behavior were any indication of his home life, her guess was that his wife was not a happy woman.

"What a sad, wretched man," she thought, her heart dropping a little at this discovery.

"At least I have James," she thought, circumnavigating the pain that often comes with empathy. He was a decent guy. Hardworking. Wanted the best for everyone and sent Christmas cards to his half-sister in Malibu, even though they hadn't talked in years. True, their sex life had dwindled over the six years they'd been living together. "But that happens to all couples, right?" she thought. He worked during the day and she worked nights, so finding the time and energy to "get it on" wasn't high on either of their priority lists.

Then it suddenly hit her; they'd been living separate lives—together. Heaviness washed over Diana. A thick ball pressed into her throat as she thought back to the first sweet months of their relationship. How they couldn't get enough of each other. How sex seemed like an endless erotic playground: the light tickles on the back of her fingers while barely touching the hairs on his cheek; his front teeth slowly biting down on her nipple until a sharp, painful rush of heat rolled over her breasts; the electric current pulsing through the tips of their tongues when they lingered in a kiss.

The heaviness gave way to hollowness. A black void opened in her chest that travelled to her belly before shifting downward.

"When was the last time I had my pussy touched? Or even looked at, for that matter?" she wondered.

The thick ball in her throat rose. Her face flushed. Internal pressure built in her forehead to the point where she could no longer control the tears swelling in her eyes.

"It's just been a long night," she lied. The tears quelled for a moment, though her fingers started to tremble. In that black void sat a burning, unavoidable truth.

She'd had enough. And not just with that night. With everything. Her life felt somehow empty. She filled her days with house cleaning and catching up on sleep, while her nights consisted of emotionally managing men with painfully unquenchable thirsts.

"What happened to *my* thirst?" she wondered. "What about my, what? Hunger? Am I like one of those people who hasn't eaten in so long that they forgot what hunger feels like?"

A far rumble of thunder brought her back to the present. She looked to the southwest and noticed a ragged band of low clouds forming in the distance.

"Shit," she whispered.

Glancing around, she took note of the nearest reinforced structures should the weather turn ugly fast. Unfortunately, they were all shuttered. Nothing else existed in the area beyond the bar, except a bridal shop—which certainly wasn't open at that time of morning—and a cemetery.

In her search for shelter, she noticed a masculine-looking Shadow not twenty feet away from her. Her defenses instantly snapped into place, like a puffer fish flaring its blades. Who was he? How long had he been there? She checked her watch. 4:30am. Had he been watching her this whole time?

Diana started walking. Quickly. Her body buzzed on high alert, and she held her breath as she rushed down the street. Her feet scraped carelessly along the sidewalk, leaving a jagged, scratching sound in their wake. Behind her beat the brisk, steady rhythm of heel to cement.

In a desperate effort to barricade herself from the Shadow, she flew towards the bridal shop on her right, where she'd spent many nights gazing longingly at its display of layered, white organza. Her hope for a miracle evaporated as she jostled the door handle. It didn't budge.

Noticing the Shadow's quick approach, Diana headed towards the cemetery. She rarely went there. Seeing her father's grave—perennially marked with a small American flag—left her feeling empty. The futility of his death had carved a hole in her life. Regardless, avoiding her father's ghost wasn't a priority in that moment. She knew the groundskeeper lived on the other side, and if she could make it to his place in time, she could wait out the storm and hopefully deter her Shadow.

She raced to the iron gate affixed between two, twelve-foot high, rectangular pillars of cement. She gripped the bars and pulled the door towards her. It didn't move. Cursing under her breath, she quickly located the latch handle but lost precious seconds wrestling with it as a hot wind whipped her hair into her eyes. She felt the clouds pressing on her back. The storm was gaining on her.

She wiped her hair out of her face and glanced behind her, nearly freezing when she saw him only three long strides away. Remembering to move her legs, she slipped inside the gate, but as she tried to close the door on her Shadow, he caught it in time and swung it open, sending her nearly flat on her back. She regained her footing and turned to run, but didn't make it more than four steps before one arm gripped around her waist, pinning her limbs to her body, and another arm wrapped around her shoulder to cover her mouth. Her usual strength and agility were no match for the hulking Shadow surrounding her.

They stood suspended in eternity. Her pelvis pressed firmly into the hard angles of his hips. His belly methodically inhaled into her spine, while she struggled to manage the chaotic symphony of her rasping chest. His fingers held her mouth slightly agape, and she could taste the salty, acidic wetness of his palm. The hot moisture of his breath tickled her left ear and raised the hair on her scalp. Sweat dripped down the nape of her neck, over her shoulders to the front, and down between her breasts.

Eventually, her rigidity gave way, and she surrendered limply into the warmth of his body. Diana knew she was outmatched in strength, but she hoped if she waited long enough, she would catch his weakness.

"Good girl," he whispered, feeling the shift within her to submission.

He guided her towards a mausoleum dimly lit by the streetlamp—which continued to buzz in one continuous hum. They turned into the tomb, and he pressed her face-first into the corner made by the entrance and the left wall. The heady scent of wet limestone and stale mushrooms nearly asphyxiated her. He spun her around and they were, for the first time, face to face. As suddenly as the Shadow had ambushed Diana, he abruptly released her. He stepped backward into the tomb's entrance—the glow from the dying streetlamp creating enough light for her to make out his features in the dark.

She instantly recognized him. He had started coming around the bar a few months prior. Late 40's. Red hair. Fairly good-looking. He had paralysis like Bell's Palsy that afflicted the right side of his mouth—though that didn't diminish his attractiveness to her. He always sat at the left edge of the bar, where the wood started to curve away from the main stretch. He never talked to anyone and never drew attention to himself. She never asked for his name and never thought much about him. The one thing that stuck with her, though, was his curious habit of only ordering soda water with lime, which she always found untouched at the end of the night.

Infused with fear, curiosity and bewilderment, Diana pressed herself against the wall, unsure whether to face the Shadow within the tomb or brave the brewing storm outside the mausoleum walls.

"I know you know me, Diana," he said, trying to mollify her as he read her thoughts through the changing expressions on her face. "I've been paying attention to you. I see how miserable you are. I know you want more—so much more."

She stood there, fascinated, vacillating between repulsion and unspeakable attraction. Who the arrogant *fuck* did he think he was? How long had this creep been watching her? How did he know *anything* about what she wanted?

And why was she suddenly hungering for him to pull her deeper into him? Electricity swirled up from her feet, legs, thighs, chest and finally washed over her face. Despite the enveloping darkness, she was positive he noticed the reddening of her cheeks. Something in her hated him for that—for feeling her so deeply without asking permission. And yet, another part of her—some dormant appetite—wanted him to feel her even more.

He stared at her face. She wasn't sure if he was contemplating what to do with her or if he was simply curious about her features. His gaze was intense, but she stayed with him. Though her nerves were still on high alert, she didn't want to miss a moment of his attention.

He lifted a finger and hovered it near her temple.

"May I?" he asked, his unquestionable authority now replaced by a sincere longing.

Surprised he would ask permission, yet unsure of his intentions, she waited a moment before responding.

"No," she replied firmly in a steady voice.

Obediently, he refrained from touching her, but he didn't move away either. The electricity between them thickened, as neither dared to move.

After an aching eternity, the Shadow asked again, "May I?"

She tuned in to her heart once more and again she replied with a solid, "No."

The showdown between them continued, as they held their mutual stance: Diana standing straight against the wall and the Shadow floating just beyond the length of his beard.

The growing wind whistled through the cracks in the walls as a brutal chill overtook her. She knew he could feel it, too. Shaking, they held still, vibrating in unison as their collective cold sweat dripped upon the earth.

Finally, without waiting for him to ask again and as if obeying some otherworldly compulsion, she simply said, "Yes."

The Shadow moved in to touch her, but before he could, she quickly amended her terms.

"But only move when I say you can."

He nodded his understanding and placed his finger on her slippery skin. The potency of this single touch nearly blew her back against the wall. He held still, waiting for her signal.

"Go on," she breathlessly whispered.

He traced his finger over the arch of her brow, down her cheek and along the edge of her jaw. She winced in anticipation when he stroked the gash on her neck but felt no pain. He furrowed his brow and peered into her eyes, again asking for permission. She nodded her head once, and he brought his mouth down to her neck. He drew the tip of his tongue along the wound. She surrendered to his touch.

Rain began to fall in shimmering sheets outside the catacomb, ricocheting off the ground and splashing on her bare legs. Stinging chills prickled over her whole body, but she remained still.

"Mmm," he murmured. "I want to taste all of you." His words reverberated through her body, softening any lingering hesitancy.

He bent his misshapen mouth to hers. Diana lapped up the cool, irresistible freshness of his kiss, like cold lemon water in the desert. She reached her tongue further into his mouth. She wanted to consume him—and at the same time, she wanted him to consume her. To suck him deeper into her. To envelope his flesh with hers.

He pulled his mouth away. Hungrily, she grabbed his hand and skimmed it down her chest and over her abdomen. He unbuttoned her black jean shorts and slipped his hand down the front. He paused, once again awaiting Diana's invitation. She gruffly pulled him closer to her, demanding that he keep going.

His first two fingers curled in and slowly slid into her. The thick, heavy wetness dripped from between her legs into his palm. Her walls ached and pulsed around him. He felt her yearning, but the sadist within him kept her bound in the chasm between her wanting and her satisfaction. Suspended in that temporal abyss, she would have normally rushed towards a hard fuck. But something so new, so different, so expansive filled her. She didn't dare move a muscle.

Unhurried, he pulled out of her—the ridges of his dry, cracked fingers reading the words written on her walls like living braille. He brought his forefinger towards his face, brushed it against his mouth and then, in one single move, placed it on his tongue, wrapped his lips around it and pulled it out, sucking all her juice. He then took his middle finger and brought it near her mouth. She licked her lips and invitingly opened them wider. He slid his finger into her mouth. A rush of sweet, salty warmth cascaded over her tongue. He drew his finger out while she lingered in the taste of herself.

After a moment, she opened her eyes to find his lopsided smile reflecting back at her.

"So?" he asked.

"Yes," she whispered.

"Yes?"

"Yes."

"No."

Diana blinked in confusion. No? He was telling her no? No to what? Why was he there if not to fuck her? She wanted him. He clearly wanted her.

The Shadow stepped towards the entrance, pale light once again illuminating his frame. It was only then that Diana saw it: a wound perfectly mirroring her own stretched across the side of his neck. She gasped in fear and amazement and when her hand instinctively flew to her neck to cover the gash, his movements simultaneously copied hers. They breathed in unison, a perfect reflection of each other.

Reading the emotional storm through her silent expressions, he softly laughed and said, "This is how I always want to remember you. Hungry. Open. Vulnerable. Consumed by desire. I want every moment of your life to be this electric. This alive."

And, as quickly as he had come upon her, he made his escape into the chilly rain, now falling even heavier. His sudden departure knocked her off balance and sent her plummeting to the ground. Unwilling to let the Shadow go, she crawled through the dirt towards the exit. But as she peered around the corner, all she saw were faded granite tombstones and American flags unevenly scattered across the field. One headstone attracted her eye with its perfectly symmetrical ring of marigolds placed before it. Lightning flashed before her, cascading across a grayish-green sky, as the winds gained in intensity. Any trace of her Shadow lover seemed to have been washed into non-existence.

A cold wind blasted across her eyes, forcing her to recoil back into the mausoleum. She glued herself to the wall as the tornado's telltale roar quickly grew in volume. The coolness of the wet stone was no match for the heat coursing through her body.

"Who or what was that?" Diana wondered. She listened intently as the twister grew louder. "Should I go after him? Should I go home? How *could* I go home? Is it possible to go back? Do I *want* to go back?"

Her thoughts collided until she couldn't focus any more. She huddled on the ground as emptiness swelled from the earth and overtook her. Leaves, shredded bits of flag and other detritus blew past the tomb's opening. She listened in howling deafness as the twister swirled around her. It pounded and shook the walls as her terror grew. She curled her fingers into the earth, gripping with futility upon the loose soil.

Then, like a beacon within her turbulent mind, she suddenly recalled a line from years ago (tenth grade English?) that brought everything into perfect focus: *Even if they're a crowd of sorrows, who violently sweep your house empty of its furniture, still treat each guest honorably.*

Gary's words finally fell into place, like puzzle pieces interlocking: *You—like her—are just a guest house. You too will die. Don't let it be in this place.* Choosing to die with honor, she relaxed her fingers and extended her arms, inviting the violent crowd of sorrows to sweep through her. Knowing she was defeated, she fell face down upon the earth. The cacophony surrounding her continued to blow, even as her perception of it faded to a soundless emptiness. Her mind blanked and she remained still, dead to the world, until the twister swiftly dissipated and the clouds parted, revealing the dawn.

When she finally opened her eyes, the truth of who Diana was hung undeniably on the nascent daylight piercing through the tomb's entrance. With uncompromising determination, she made her choice: she would follow the path opening before her.

No, she would not be meeting JB at the bar at 4:30. No, she would not be returning home to James. No, she would not be confined by the walls of that town. And no, she would not be running away from her hunger anymore.

As the minutes passed, Diana felt her cells settle back into her skin, and she stood with her feet firmly connected to the earth beneath her. She wiped the dirt off her face with the back of her hand, headed out of the crypt and marched towards the cemetery gate—passing the circle of marigolds which had remained untouched. Exiting the iron door, Diana noticed the empty foundation that now occupied the space where the bridal shop once stood. Now grateful for the shop's locked door, Diana inhaled deeply as if she could breathe for the first time, the fragrant petrichor slaking her thirsty senses. The crisp morning greeted her limpid eyes. She was awake. And even though her certainty wavered, wondering if what she was doing was right, she did know that it felt true—which was all the confirmation she needed.

As Diana looked north towards the open road, she caught a final glimpse of the little bar on the edge of town—the only town she had ever known. The last thing she saw before turning her back was the single streetlamp, now no longer flickering but burning brightly against the white-hot glow of the rising sun.

the queen archetype
POWER, SURRENDER

> *Something amazing happens when we surrender*
> *and just love. We melt into another world,*
> *a realm of power already within us.*
> *~ Marianne Williamson*

The Queen Archetype is the expression of feminine power and leadership. She rules in service to her court, which can resemble anything from a corporation to a home to a book club. The Queen is often thought of as someone with ultimate authority. While that may be true on some level, a true Queen knows that her power comes from surrendering to what will best serve her subjects. She does not demand obeisance—she simply rests in grace.

Due to the overwhelming patriarchal fear of women's power, however, we often see Queens in fairy tales and history books depicted as wicked, controlling, and demanding punishment for their subjects at the slightest infraction. The Queen is usually described as old and ugly in comparison to her virtuous nemesis, the young and meek maiden who epitomizes purity and goodness. If the Queen happens to be beautiful, moreover, she is often riddled with vanity and jealousy of other women.

A true Queen is loving and espouses generosity that stems from her capacity to receive. No matter the circumstances, she is a woman who knows how to open her arms and live in abundance. Because she lives her life from a place of fullness rather than lack, the Queen is surrounded by riches—and she is generally happy to give.

There is a maturity and stillness that rests in the center of the Queen. She possesses a keen charisma, much like the Whore. However, unlike the Whore, she uses gravity rather than seduction. In the erotic sense, she is a woman that people *want* to serve. It gives her subjects great pleasure to offer themselves to her because they know she will either revel with delight in their services or lovingly ask for an adjustment in their communication or behavior.

Sexually, this is a woman who knows her worth and what she wants. She won't fuck someone just to make him or her like her; she will do it because it is her desire. While she has no problem making a request, at the same time, she relishes improvisation, spontaneity, and unexpected delights found within the present moment.

the shadow queen

One shadow version of the Queen archetype is the Tyrant. She is petty, insecure, and driven by the fear that someone is always looking to depose her. If she senses the slightest hint of mutiny, she screams, "Off with his head!" She is constantly proving her authority and using aggression and control to attain respect, rather than simply trusting her own power.

The Princess is another shadow of the Queen. Instead of receiving her abundance with gratitude, she approaches it with a sense of entitlement. Within the Princess is an immature, spoiled brat who is rarely satisfied with what she has. When her subjects run out of bread, the Princess obliviously declares, "Let them eat cake." She cares only for her own self-centered comfort and whims.

integrated and shadow examples of the queen

- Cleopatra: Last ruler of Ptolemaic Egypt before it became part of the Roman Empire.
- Hera: Queen of the Greek gods. Co-ruler of Mount Olympus with Zeus.
- Jezebel: Though reviled in Judeo-Christian mythology, she was a smart, cultured, and outspoken Phoenician princess who married King Ahab of the Northern Kingdom (Israel). Her tainted legacy may be based more in racism and misogyny than her own treachery.
- Oprah Winfrey: Television talk show Queen who has built a media empire.
- Queen Ana Nzinga: Seventeenth-century Angolan queen who fought and negotiated with the Portuguese conquerors.
- Queen Rania: The current queen of Jordan, who is a fierce advocate for education, health, and women's rights.

- Evil Queen in Snow White (Tyrant Shadow).
- Queen of Hearts in *Alice in Wonderland* (Tyrant Shadow).
- The clique of popular girls in *Mean Girls* (Princess Shadow).

inviting the queen into our lives

The Queen isn't afraid to ask for what she wants; more importantly, she's not afraid to receive. Speaking our sexual desires already brings up a host of emotions—but sitting still and surrendering into those desires is the mark of a true Queen. Power exchange is a fun and safe way to tap into that regal essence. We can practice telling our partner(s) what we want, then let them take over as they fulfill our desires. It's important to notice the ways we try to micromanage a situation. If guidance is needed, of course, offer it. But when our minds constantly seek ways to criticize, it keeps us from fully surrendering into the moment—cutting us off from our own power.

The Queen teaches us to own and unapologetically *claim* our power, while at the same time wielding it with grace, compassion, and responsibility. When we connect to our desire and trust that we are worthy of it, we no longer walk around like starving Princesses or Tyrants demanding that the world bow at our feet. We simply find our deep "Yes" within the bounty and benevolence of life and, with the serene majesty of royalty, take our rightful place upon the throne.

fairy tales

From your perspective
It must seem as easy as
Drawing the sword from the stone
Or soaring on a magic carpet
Or spinning straw into gold.

But I know myself.

Princesses only stay pure
Through obstinate abstinence.

So you'll find me in the gutter—
Cigarette in one hand,
Ice cream in the other—
And marvel at how easily angels fall.

But if you're brave enough to climb my tower
(And make friends with the sleeping dragon)
Then don't try to explain me
(Your tongue has better uses).

Strip off your armor
(Women aren't won with steel)
And succumb to the tumbling embers
From the beast (no longer tame)
As you rouse beauty from her slumber
With a kiss of fairy flame.

After all
(As Rilke says)
Perhaps all the dragons in our lives
Are princesses
Who are only waiting to see us act
(Just once)
With beauty and courage.

rani

Rani placed the edge of the chilled glass against her slightly parted lips and tipped back her head. Bright bubbles tickled the back of her throat, while the dry, cherry flavor of the 2005 Cristal Rosé Brut washed over her tongue. She closed her eyes, savoring the cool relief from the unusually hot October afternoon. After the champagne had sufficiently slaked her thirst, she set the flute down on the cream and gold-colored cocktail napkin. She glanced down at her Richard Mille 007 rose gold watch, given to her exactly one year ago for her 44th birthday.

"Twelve twenty-eight," she noted, the hands pointing towards two small diamonds representing the clock face's twelve and six.

She remembered the e-mail verbatim:

Alley
Sit at the bar
12:30 SHARP
Wear a dress
Xo, Ms. V

She re-crossed her legs, feeling the smooth cushion of the suede barstool as it brushed against her bare thighs. She hooked the left heel of her Louboutin black-and-crystal pump on the bottom rung of her seat.

"Twelve twenty-nine."

Admiring the artist's penmanship, she softly fingered the paper "Reserved" sign that sat three inches behind her glass.

The R snaked under the rest of the word in thick calligraphy. A similar yet scripturally unique sign sat nine inches to her left, saving the empty space next to her. A smartly-dressed woman in royal blue sipped a Queen's Cocktail on Rani's right.

"Good thing Ms. V had the foresight to reserve us a spot," Rani thought, as she glanced around the packed restaurant. "But then again, she's a stickler for details."

Ever since Alley opened near Gramercy Park a little over a year and a half ago, it had been the hot spot for New York City's wealthy and elite. Rani could count on it to "wow" her potential investors and business contacts. And she adored the care and attention put into every detail of the place. The décor, the cuisine, the wines, the gold-plated napkin rings and handwritten menus—all of it represented simple yet elegant tastes while fostering a welcome atmosphere. She couldn't help but step inside the intimacy of her experience, even as she sat sliding her long fingers up and down the stem of her flute. Supple flesh on firm glass.

No sooner had Rani drifted off than she was startled by the appearance of a stranger in the seat beside her. She quickly looked at her watch.

"Twelve-thirty? That was only a minute?!" she thought, surprised at how quickly she had lost her sense of temporal perception.

"Excuse me, sir," she said, "this seat's reserved."

"I know," he replied, a smile curling around his mouth.

Rani sharply focused her eyes on him and took in the mysterious interloper for the first time. Mid-to-late 50's. Handsome face, with strong lines and signs of aging that proved he had not had an uneventful youth. He was on the shorter side, with a thick build. His olive skin glowed under a mop of jet-black hair, flecked with silver wisps. His manicured hands looked wide and warm, neatly framed by sable-colored suit sleeves pinned with onyx cufflinks. He casually tucked his right hand into his jacket pocket while his left mischievously stroked his lightly-stubbled chin. He wore a black shirt and solid black necktie. His shoes, too, were black leather, and she could make out an interlacing pattern sewn into the top of them.

But what captured her attention most were his eyes: two blue-gray pools penetrated her with a stare that was almost too indecent for polite company. They stood out in stark relief against the dark backdrop that formed the rest of him.

"Well?" he asked, the grin winding across his lips.

She realized she'd been gaping at him for several seconds. Extracting herself from his magnetic void, she looked at her glass and regained her composure before speaking.

"I'm just not used to people being so forward with me. While I'm flattered, I have to tell you that I am both waiting for someone and in a relationship."

"I know," he repeated.

Again, she froze.

"Who are you?"

"I'm an envoy of Ms. V," he replied.

"Oh!" exclaimed Rani in sudden recognition.

"My instructions were simply to bring you to your limits of surrender."

"Oh," whispered Rani with trepidation.

In their time together, Ms. V had created some outrageous and unpredictable scenes with Rani: the time she flew Rani out to Rome to make love to her in the Coliseum after hours, even with the Italian guards standing only twenty feet away. They made it only ten minutes before being thrown out, but they laughed with girlish delight all the way back to New York.

Or the time they seduced a waiter in Paris and spent hours deliciously torturing him by tying him up so that he couldn't touch himself as he watched Ms. V delight in Rani's tangy, sweet taste.

But this was different. Ms. V had been present for all of their playful experiences. She'd never been passed into another's control.

Rani pressed her fingers into her eyes, trying to make sense of his words.

"So," she whispered in hushed tones, "you're here *alone*?"

"Yes."

Her stomach dropped.

"Are you a professional?"

"Hmmm, something like that," he replied, amused by her nervous questioning.

She nodded, his voice pinging around her brain like a loose pinball.

"Look," he added, trying to comfort her apprehension, "I have no personal agenda. I respect all boundaries. I am here only in service to your desire. The only rule I have is that you must trust me."

Trust was not something Rani granted easily—especially to men. She'd felt betrayed when those she loved pushed her away for not conforming to their standards: her brother mocking her for trying to do "a man's job;" her father disapproving that she had not chosen marriage; her lovers complaining when work mattered more than they did. She had fought hard—alone—to rise to the top in her world.

So for this stranger to come in and demand instant trust, it pushed against her edges uncomfortably—and Ms. V knew that. It took over a year of seduction before Rani succumbed to her charms. Despite all the attraction and long nights discussing sex and love and the universe over empty bottles of wine, Rani still held obstinately to her resistance.

So this 45th birthday present was not only a gift, it was a challenge. She turned her gaze back to the dark man, who was staring at her with unnerving patience.

"What is your name?" she asked, sipping her champagne.

"You may call me 'Sir,'" he curtly replied.

Rani almost spit into her glass.

"Really?" she laughed. "You don't think that's a little too 'on the nose'?"

"It's worked for me so far," he said.

"Okay, Sir," she said, sarcasm dripping.

"When you learn the art of surrender, names are irrelevant."

Rani paused at his statement, initially because it seemed tritely ripped out of the pages of *Fifty Shades*. But when she put aside her prejudice and dropped into the weight of its meaning, she wondered about her own capacity to surrender. She had come a long way from the days where she would let guys fuck her hard and fast just so she could get it over with. She had tasted unimaginable realms of pleasure, much of it at the hands of another woman—something she had never considered exploring until her late thirties.

But here Rani was, dangling on the cusp of another abyss. All she had to do was take the leap.

"Would you like something to drink?" she asked, trying to regain her sense of control and attempting to stall the conversation.

"No thanks," he courteously replied. "All I want is your 'Yes.'"

She inhaled sharply as a rush of heat swelled, ran down her body and pooled between her thick thighs.

"Fuck!" she thought. As much as she was trying to deflect his advances, her body was giving away her wanting.

"Look," he said, cutting to the chase, "I only have sixty minutes with you. That's it. So you can tell me, now, to leave, and I will respect that. Or you can come with me and let me do what I do best. The choice is yours. But I need an answer now. Ms. V specifically instructed me not to let you stall."

Fury coursed through Rani, mingling with the fervor of her own desire. She couldn't believe the gall of Ms. V. Well, she could. But this? This was asking too much.

"Fuck her," Rani thought in rebellion. "Fuck her and all her 'knowing what's best.' She wants me to do this? FINE. Let's just see if this asshole has what it takes."

"Yes," she declared; an air of defiance permeated beyond their isolated bubble. The well-dressed woman in blue next to Rani glanced over with curiosity.

He smiled lasciviously.

"Good," he said. He leaned over, his lips resting next to the edge of her ear, and whispered, "Just so you know, I like 'em a little insubordinate. It makes the game more fun."

Rani's face flushed. Caught in the heat of their exchange, she didn't notice her heel slipping off the barstool's wooden rail. Her hands flung out and clutched onto his shirt, breaking her fall and simultaneously planting her face in his chest.

"Well that's a good start," he laughed, gripping her by the arms and bringing her to her feet.

She smoothed down her rising skirt, grabbed her snakeskin clutch and glanced around the restaurant with embarrassment, hoping that no one caught her momentary misstep. Only the woman sitting next to Rani seemed to be smiling inconspicuously.

After gathering her floundering dignity once more, Rani asked with as much sangfroid as she could muster, "Where to next?"

"The bathroom," he replied evenly. "The one on the far left. Go there now. Take care of any needs. In exactly three minutes, you will hear me knock three times, like this."

He rapped his knuckles against the mahogany bar in a slow, decisive beat.

"Got it?"

She nodded her assent.

"Good. I'll pick up the tab here. See you in three."

Dazed, Rani floated through the maze of servers, tables and chairs. She made her way to the darkened hall in the back, near the VIP lounge. Amber floor lights glowed, guiding her way. Finally, she arrived at her destination. The piece of her that had hoped the room would already be occupied vaporized to smoke when she saw the handwritten sign affixed to the door.

Out of Service

"Fuck. That woman thinks of everything."

She placed her hand on the long, metal handle. Icy chills ran through her fingertips, while a blazing fever flushed her cheeks. She took a deep breath, and without thinking, she whipped open the door, slammed it shut and turned the metal latch. Rani pressed her forehead and palms against the door, willing her body to stand up against the impending vertigo.

Trying to stabilize her spinning senses, she deliberately turned around and took in her surroundings. For as many times as she'd been to Alley, she had never noticed the powder room before. It was enormous. Red and amber lights hummed near the floor, emitting a soft incandescence similar to the lounge and hallway. A suede lounge chair sat in the corner to the right, its color reminding her of the caramel-colored cushion of the barstools. A clear, bowled sink sat upon a shiny, obsidian stand. Both the toilet and bidet were a glossy black, their gold-plated handles reflecting the warm glow of the lights.

Staring directly at her was a large, framed print of the iconic *Tournée du Chat Noir* poster, hanging between the bidet and the sink. The cat's hedonistic eyes bore into Rani's. She shivered, averting her gaze.

After the internal whirling of her cells came to a standstill, she dared to peek down at her watch.

Five…four…three…two…one.

Still leaning against the door, Rani felt three measured knocks reverberate through her body.

"Just a minute," she cried, realizing she hadn't yet gone to the bathroom.

Knock. Knock. Knock.

Again, he rapped against the door, his firmness escalating—indicating his displeasure at her delay. Without wasting another second, she unlocked the door and pulled it open. He stood perfectly in the center of the archway, fist still raised in the air and arrogant smile painted on his dark face.

"I hate him," she thought. "I absolutely hate this motherfucker."

"Happy to see you, too," he replied, reading her mind, which only fueled her growing fury. He sauntered past her in two long strides, careful not to touch her. He then pivoted so he faced her back. His body hummed only inches from hers.

"Close the door," he whispered, his breath caressing her naked shoulders.

Hypnotized, she reached for the handle and pulled the door shut.

"Lock it."

Click.

"Turn around."

Rani shifted in place until her shoulders were square to his.

"Look at me."

She lifted her gaze until her dark eyes met his blue-gray orbs. She could see her face reflected in those infinite mirrors. His pupils dilated as his hungry stare took her in.

"Breathe," he prompted.

She smirked, realizing that she'd been breathing erratically since he sat down next to her at the bar. She softened her shoulders and closed her eyes, preparing to inhale.

"Look at me," he repeated softly. "Stay connected."

Rani focused on him once more, let go of her belly and drank in the cool air, clearing her stagnant lungs.

"Again."

He mirrored her breath this time as she breathed again. She felt thick heat dropping down through her legs once more. Her fingertips pulsed with a rhythm matching that of her own accelerating heart.

"May I touch your shoulders?" he asked.

She blinked, shocked by the recognition that he had not yet touched her voluntarily—only to help her gain her footing after her awkward tumble off the barstool.

"Y-yes," she replied.

He firmly placed his palms on the curve of her bare shoulders and lightly pressed down. She sunk towards the floor.

"Once more. Breathe."

Locking his gaze, Rani eased into his touch and felt his hands rise and fall as the air gently swept into her hollow chest.

"Perfect," he said. "How do you feel?"

"Okay," she answered. "More relaxed."

"Good," he replied, dropping his hands. She felt a twinge of regret that he didn't remain physically connected to her longer. She yearned for the stranger's warm skin on hers once more.

"My understanding is that you know and use safe words? Red, yellow, green?"

Rani nodded, his abrupt change in conversation bringing her back from her nostalgic fantasy.

"Good. And I understand your tests came up negative. So have mine."

Rani's face turned red. Though she trusted Ms. V and appreciated her care, it was still disconcerting that a complete stranger had access to this intimate knowledge while Rani knew very little about him.

"Boundaries?"

She silently shook her head.

"You have *no* boundaries?" he asked with a dubious look.

"W-well," she stammered, "I don't like a *whole* lot of pain, though some is fine—and I need a lot of warm up before certain, um, penetrations?" She paused, unclear of where to go next. She didn't know this man—or how far he was willing to go.

"Slapping? Punching? Spanking?" he prodded.

"No punching," she emphasized.

"Of course," he noted.

"What are *your* boundaries?" she asked, hoping to glean a bit more information about him.

"No scat, no permanent marks—and I never take anyone further than they want to go."

"Then why are you here?" challenged Rani. He looked at her quizzically. "I mean, what's the point of doing all this if you're only going to take people where they've already been?"

A knowing smile crossed his face.

"Because, my dear, most people haven't begun to test the edges of their wanting. It challenges their perfectly constructed reality of who they think they are. Or those who dare to dream that more is possible don't believe someone exists who could take them there. So most people won't bother to seek it out."

He leaned in closer, his lips almost touching hers as he whispered, "But you're not most people, are you, Rani?"

A thick charge hung in the air between them as the truth of his words sunk into her. He could sense her acquiescence: the shifting of her legs that lessened the distance between them, her willingness to hold his steady gaze, the way she involuntarily licked her parting lips.

"So, I think we're ready, yes?" he asked.

She nodded her head in agreement.

"Are you sure?"

She nodded once more.

"Say it out loud."

"Yes. I am ready," she spoke, determined and firm in her desire.

"Understood. Thank you." He walked over to the lounge chair, grabbed a cushion and placed it next to the wall.

"Kneel down, facing me," he instructed. The seductive melody he'd crooned only moments before was replaced with a harsher tone that carried a firm authoritarian edge.

Rani obeyed, even though his sharp directness made her uneasy. Hiking up the skirt of her wine-colored Hervé Léger cocktail dress, she dropped down towards the cushion, using the wall to brace her descent.

He ferreted around his breast pocket for a moment before pulling out a black band of cloth.

"Put this on."

Taking it from his hands, she saw it was a blindfold. She placed the elastic band at the back of her skull and covered her face with the wide fabric, sheathing her eyes. With her vision compromised, the rest of her senses suddenly awoke. She noticed the blindfold's plush softness—like terry cloth treated with fabric softener. It smelled of aftershave and orange. She heard the quickening of his breath and the rustle of his jacket against itself. The astringent bite from the rosé lingered on her breath.

Only a few moments had passed since she donned the blindfold, but the thick blackness swallowed her whole, submerging her into a surrendered dream state.

Sensing her readiness, he bent over her and caressed her head. She softened at his gentle touch. He stroked the back of his fingers on her warming cheeks before skimming his nails over her *décolletage*. She softened into his unexpected sweetness.

He then slid his hand up the back of her neck and grabbed the thick, black hair at her nape. Pulling her ear towards his mouth, he whispered, "Give me your tongue."

She opened her mouth. He knelt before her and hungrily pressed his face to hers. He tasted of peppermint and coffee. His lips were thick and wet, and though he was ravenously delighting in her, he was also careful to keep his kisses subtly restrained. She appreciated his skill of discernment. It was inviting—like there was space for more of her to come out.

His kisses moved over her chin, down her throat to her collarbones and finally to the tops of her nearly exposed breasts. He slowly traced his tongue near the edge where her skin met the dress. Then in one swift move, he freed her left nipple and gripped it between his teeth.

"Ah!" cried Rani, not expecting the sudden sharpness. Yet the intensity of the sensation sent a bolt of electricity down to her anticipating pussy.

She paused briefly at this realization. Although he'd only been touching her for about a minute, she was surprised at how wet she was. Shaking off any pretense, she gave in to her desire and arched her back, presenting more of herself to his voracious mouth.

He worked his way over her belly and hips before landing between her thighs, his hot breath warming her flesh through the fabric. She could feel his hands sliding down the curve of her ass and resting shortly thereafter at the bottom edge of the dress. He curled his fingers under the skirt and grazed them over her silk panties. She sank down, yearning for more pressure from his touch. Sensing her earnestness, he yanked his hand from under her and firmly cupped her chin.

"Uh-uh-uh," he singsonged. "Not yet." Teasingly, he drew his hand under the base of her nose. She could smell her own muskiness on his fingertips. He ran his fingers down her face and inserted them into her mouth. As he began to draw them in and out, she tightened her lips around him.

"Fuck," he groaned as she pulled him in, deeper and deeper. He jerked his fingers away from her mouth, kissed her hard and whispered, "I want you to suck me."

He swiftly rose. Rani heard the metal clasp from his belt clinking against the buckle as he undid his pants. She held her breath as the lingering quiet fed her impatient madness. Finally, he grabbed her hand, spat into her palm and wrapped it around his cock. The slick slip of the latex condom stroked her skin.

"Stay steady," he guided, keeping his hand on hers as he slowly moved his hips forward and back. The more delicate and focused her touch, the more he hardened. He sped up for only a fraction of a second before slowing down to an achingly slow pace.

"I'm going to release you now. Keep your hand on the base of my cock and put me in your mouth."

Rani was surprised and a little affronted at his frank instructions.

"This isn't the first time I've sucked a dick," she internally rebelled. But she quelled her animus and chose to appreciate the vulnerability of a man trusting her with his desire. She took him in her mouth. Saliva built along the walls of her cheeks, and she used her tongue to lubricate his shaft. When he was liberally wet, she made feathery flicks on the underbelly of his cock, then ran the tip of her tongue just under its head, feeling the pulses of tight, little ridges.

He brought his hand to the top of her head once more and gripped her hair, yielding to the back of her throat. They rested there, suspended for several moments. Her throat contracted, sending undulating pulsations through the tip of his cock.

He pulled out and oceans of fluid spilled from her mouth.

"Did he cum?" she wondered, tasting the wetness. Then she remembered he was wearing a condom. "No, it's me. My saliva. Down my face. My neck. My pretty designer dress. My very *expensive* designer dress."

"Put this on," he instructed, handing her a latex glove and snapping her from her sartorial lamentations.

"Lick my balls and finger my ass," he demanded.

Rani choked. Ass play wasn't her thing—plus she'd never been on the *giving* side of the equation. But, without protestation, she clumsily wrestled on the glove, blindly felt her way to the soft, hirsute pouch behind his cock and enveloped him with her lips. Course scratchiness—though not unpleasant—tickled her mouth. She lingered, using her fingers to guide more of him into her.

She then reached her right forefinger behind the curve of his perineum and slowly circled his asshole. She felt his muscles drop down around her fingertip and open to her touch. She easily slipped two-thirds of her saliva-lubricated finger inside him.

They remained still once more—dangling on an expectant precipice. After a moment, he reached down and stroked her cheek. His caress was warm and tender. She leaned a fraction more into his touch. Taking his sweetness as a sign to return to his cock, Rani freed her left hand and wrapped it around his shaft, bringing him to her lips. She lightly kissed his head, her tongue occasionally grazing him.

Then, without warning, he rammed the entire length of his cock into her mouth. She tensed at the sudden intrusion—but in spite of the gagging, the barely breathing, the eyes and nose watering, she kept opening wider and wider to hold all of him. All of them.

He slammed into her again. Again. And again. Over and over. She tightened her throat, held her breath and steeled herself against him. But once she could no longer stave off her gag reflex, she yanked her head away and disengaged from his penetrating violence. She coughed wildly as saliva and snot shot up and out of her nose. Her eyes reddened and watered. She used her hands to desperately clean her face but kept the blindfold in place.

"How are you?" he asked.

"Ok," coughed Rani as her hacking abated.

"What else?" he prodded.

"Nothing, nothing," she responded, wanting to wrap things up as soon as possible. She blindly fumbled for his cock and tried to put it back into her mouth.

"No," he said, ripping the blindfold off her face. "Speak."

"I'm fine. Let's just keep going," she said, trying to 'finish the job.'

"No, you're not fine. What do you want?" he pointedly asked.

She gaped at him, not sure how to answer.

"Speak!" he shouted again.

Once more, she remained mute.

"Fuck, woman! WHAT DO YOU WANT?"

"I'M FINE!" she finally cried back. "Really, let's just do this thing."

He eyed her for a moment, clearly determining his next step. She felt his investigative gaze sweep over her. After several seconds, Rani noticed him imperceptibly nod as the decision came to him. Without taking his eyes off her, he slipped his hands into his pockets, pulled out two latex gloves and effortlessly pulled them over his large hands.

"Remove your glove," he softly commanded.

She quickly did as she was told, keeping her eyes fixed on him.

"Take a deep breath in."

Once more she grudgingly obeyed.

"Aaaaaaaaand...exhale."

As she released her lungs, a sharp sting slashed across her left cheek and a loud crack reverberated through her ears. Involuntarily, she quickly brought her hand to the left side of her face. She blinked back tears of shock and pain. If it weren't for the evidence of his flat, open palm still lingering by her cheek, she wouldn't have believed the previous two seconds had transpired. Stunned, Rani looked at him, searching for an explanation. He simply stared at her, his eyes cold and unemotional—but not detached.

Violent rage roiled her blood. She leaned away from him and stumbled to her feet, not taking her hand away from her face. She wanted to maintain a barrier of protection should he strike again.

"What—the—fuck," she whispered, menace oozing from her.

He simply held his silence, which angered Rani even more.

"Speak, you pathetic prick!" she cried.

Again, nothing.

"FUCK YOU!" she screamed. Blinded by her fury, she grabbed the gold soap dispenser off the sink and hurled it at his head. He ducked just in time to avoid the metallic missile. It bounced off the wall behind him and clanged to the ground, breaking off the nozzle top and launching a jet of pink liquid across the floor.

He turned back to her, amusement creasing the corners of his mouth, and said, "Thank God it wasn't made of glass."

His statement infuriated her even more.

"Not only has he hit me," she thought, "now he's mocking me."

The pricking of her pride sent Rani over the edge.

"Fuck you!" she shrieked. "Fuck you! Fuck you! Fuck you! You think this is sexy? You think this is fun? This is *fucked up!* This is sadistic, you fucking dick."

She paused, verbally stunted by the complexity of emotions rising to the surface.

"What else do you have to say?" he asked, a surprising level of patience in his voice.

"What do *I* have to say?" she responded. "What the fuck do *you* have to say? You come in here to get to me surrender and you *slap* me? Where's the fucking logic in that, *huh*? Where's the *class*?"

"How do you feel about me?" he asked, egging her on.

"How do I feel?" she parroted. His inquiry confused her. Infuriated her. And reluctantly piqued her curiosity.

"I don't know," she finally replied, unsure of where he was going.

"You do know. Say it," he pressed.

Her glance darted to the cat print on the wall, her body slightly leaning towards the stoic animal as Rani yearned for escape.

"Eyes on me," he warned, taking a deliberate step towards her.

"Don't touch me!" she cried, reflexively moving away from him. She felt the hot tears of fear and embarrassment edging their way towards the brink of her lower eyelids.

"Push against me," he commanded. He placed his bent arms in front of his chest as if bracing for an attack.

"Push?" she questioned, not fully trusting him.

As if sensing her fear, he responded, "Yes. I am not going to hurt you."

Seeing the sincerity in his eyes, she placed her hands on his forearms and pushed. He leaned into her and, with very little effort, sent Rani sliding back and pinned her to the wall.

"Push!" he ordered. She knew he could feel her strength give way under the force of his arms.

She tried pushing against him again.

"PUSH, YOU FUCKING BITCH!" he cried.

Ignited by his insult, Rani thrust her hands towards him, knocking him off-balance. Once he was far enough away for her to see all of him, she inhaled down to her toes and spat in his face. Stunned by this unforeseen tactic, he stepped back and wiped her spit from his eyes. Freed, she launched her body at him, knocking him to the floor. His upper body landed on the cushion he'd placed down for her to kneel, saving them both from a hard landing. She straddled him and flung her limbs towards his chest.

She had lost any sense of kindness or compassion. All she wanted was his defeat. His total and utter annihilation. Unconcerned with any potential permanent injury to him or to her own body, she railed against him, as a primal scream tore through the heated fabric of her skin. Finally, after an eternity of disjointed rage poured from her shattering mouth, she semi-recovered her verbal capacities.

"I HATE YOU!" Rani shrieked. "I FUCKING HATE YOU AND EVERYONE LIKE YOU! ALL YOU FUCKING MEN! YOU FUCKING ARROGANT ASSHOLES. YOU WEAK, LITTLE COWARDS THAT HAVE TO USE AND ABUSE WOMEN TO MAKE YOURSELF FEEL GOOD ABOUT YOUR INSIGNIFICANT LIVES! FUCK YOU! I HATE YOU! I HATE YOU!"

She pummeled against his arms and chest until exhaustion overcame her. Slowly, her vision acclimated to the dimly lit room, and her body gave way to the heaviness of her emotions. Focusing her eyes, she could see him once more. He held his arms against his chest and face, braced against her incursion. They were covered with minor scratches and contusions, but relatively unharmed. She collapsed against him, her hot breath ripping through her lungs as she gulped for air.

Sensing that she had finished, he wrapped his arms around her and pulled her tightly against his body.

Rani melted into him as he absorbed the impact of her emotional outburst. She crushed her face, drenched with sweat, tears and snot, into his crisp, starched shirt and shook involuntarily.

"It's okay," he said softly. "I've got you. I've got you."

His words ignited a flame of desire that extended from her ears, throat, heart and belly before culminating in the dark chasm of her thick, wet pussy. Just as quickly as she had fallen into a blind rage, she now descended into a fervent carnality. She lifted her head and voraciously pressed her lips against his. Her tongue unapologetically plunged into his mouth. Her hands gripped his lapel and pulled his body towards her.

He reciprocated her libidinous advances with equal fervor and snaked his leg out from underneath her writhing body. Now freed, he wrapped it around Rani's hips and swiveled himself out from under her. She now lay on her back underneath him. She felt his erection press against her, which made her back arch, reaching for more of him. She wanted him to fuck her. Hard.

Tearing her mouth away, she looked into his eyes and said, "Fuck me now."

Without flinching, he lifted her skirt and ripped off the thin fabric of her underwear. He plunged his mouth onto her aching wetness. The pressure brought momentary relief, but she yearned to be penetrated. Her swollen pussy lips tried to suck his tongue deeper into her, but he only teased her with brief flicks on her clit. She squeezed her bare legs around his head. A fresh wave of tears peeked out from under her eyes, but this time they weren't born of pain—they were born in the underbelly of unbearable pleasure.

"Oh fuck me," Rani murmured, barely able to speak the words.

Alas, to her delighted disdain, he kept sucking at a torturous tempo, bringing her higher and higher, yet relentlessly denying her respite.

Finally, after what seemed like an agonizing eternity, she felt the hint of climax gathering in her belly. She clamped down, seeking sexual solace, but just before she plunged over the edge, he pulled his mouth away and tantalizingly blew on her clit. The cool air took her blazing heat down a notch but not enough to find relief.

"FUUUUUUUCK!!!" she cried, the wild animal of her hunger burning with fever.

He lifted his head and skirted his nose up her torso until his eyes met hers.

"I think you're ready now," he whispered, delight and mischief dancing in his words. "I want you to lick your fingers and touch your tits. But don't come."

She placed the trembling fingers of her right hand onto her tongue as she drew circles with the left around her tight and puckered nipples. The electricity from her touch shot between her legs, curling her toes. Her eyes rolled back into her head.

"Good girl," he said, stroking himself, relishing the satisfying sight of the frenzied woman squirming below him. He shifted back and placed the tip of his cock an aching two millimeters from the entrance to her pussy.

"Do you want it?" he taunted, extending his sadistic flirt a few seconds longer.

"Yes...*yes!*"

"Really?"

"YES!"

"Ask me nicely."

Rani hesitated for a moment. But then the magnitude of her desire quickly overpowered her shame and vanity. Losing control of her body, she shakily reached up and caressed his left cheek.

"Please," she cooed. "Please, enter me."

He softened to her sincerity and slowly slid inside her. She drank in the delicious fullness, relinquishing any fight she had left in her. The slick walls of her pussy descended and wrapped around him, drawing in his totality. She pulled his head towards her face and tasted the thick lusciousness of his lips. Her lips, throat, nipples, belly and the deep, deep chasm hiding in the back of her womb—everything swelled and illuminated as if some secret spell had been broken. Or perhaps remembered.

They remained still. Their hearts pulsed in sync. The polished roll of her breasts rose to meet his sinking chest as they both breathed in unison.

Then, they slowly began rocking. He held her head as he dipped her back, and she dug her fingers into his skin as they pitched forward. The subtle music of their movements echoed off the walls. She felt a deep, inward pull rising. It began below her navel, then widened out across her pelvis, thighs, shins and feet. Everything began to radiate with the gravity of her mounting orgasm. She stretched her fingers and toes outward, reaching for any last drop of sensation to add to the erotic cocktail.

She rode the edge of climax and swiftly found herself nearing the terminal peak.

Five. Four. Three. Two.

He stopped and pulled back slightly, suspending her over an infinite void. Rani peered over the edge and saw the vast expanse of her aloneness. Stark abandonment gripped her heart. She quickly cast her gaze towards him, searching for an answer, as awe and fear clouded her eyes.

"Please," she begged. "Please don't go." Any filter of pride that had remained within her was now gone. This was Rani at her most naked. Most raw. Most humble. A woman unchained from the bondages of vanity. Her unmasking freed the last vestige of Rani's control and within that freedom, she had found her true power.

She exhaled, yielding her empty mind and full body to his. As she fell limp, offering herself to death, the scent of childhood visits to Varanasi filled her nose. Marigolds. Raw milk.

Burnt flesh. He placed a finger directly onto her clit, engulfing her in electric flames and whiting out her vision.

Rani screamed as lightning bolted through them. Hot liquid jetted from her, coating his hands, arms and shirt. She plummeted into the paradoxical depths of her totality. Grotesque and majestic. Horrifying and beautiful. Greedy and gracious. Once she was wrung out by the mottled kaleidoscope of her karmic bondage, she felt all of herself, dripping and incinerated, settling into an alabaster hall of nothingness.

His perfect hands skillfully collected her thousand-and-one-colored limbs, like shattered shells in the damp sand. He pulled her in towards his chest, his shirt drenched in the mingling wetness of his sweat and her ejaculate. Sweetness rose towards her nostrils as the closeness of his body incubated the atmosphere surrounding them.

After several minutes, she peeled open her lids and stared at him blankly.

"Hi," she whispered.

"Hello," he smiled back. "Are you here?"

She laughed shyly as her eyes sharpened their focused on him.

"Yes."

"Do you need anything?" he asked.

"Um???"

"Why don't we start with cleaning you up," he suggested, shifting her near the wall and standing up. He reached for a wad of brown paper towels and handed them to her. She wiped her thighs and belly. When the paper started falling apart from the heavy wetness, he gave her some more. She smiled with a mix of gratitude and embarrassment.

After they were clean, he helped her to her feet.

"Those heels are dangerous for post-coital trekking," he said teasingly.

"But I do look great in them," she retorted playfully.

When she found her balance, she fell into his body, wrapping her arms around him in a tight embrace.

"Thank you," she said, tears gently cascading down her cheeks. "Thank you."

"My pleasure," he responded. He pulled back, looking into her sparkling, wet eyes, then dropped to his knees and kissed the tops of her feet one at a time.

Rani remained still and graciously receptive to his humility.

He rose and took her face in his hands.

"Truly, my pleasure," he repeated.

She slightly nodded, his words resonating.

He pulled his hands away and glanced at his watch.

"Well," he began, "it seems our time is up. Are you okay?"

"I'm fine," she replied.

He softly kissed her forehead then turned towards the door.

"Oh!"

He stopped, facing her once more, and said, "I almost forgot. Ms. V requested that you not eat anything until dinner tonight. She wanted the taste of us to linger in your mouth for the rest of the day."

She raised her eyebrows at the boldness of the request but quickly decided it was simply best to obey.

"Yes," said Rani.

"Good. Oh and don't worry about the mess in here. She has someone coming to take care of it."

He slid the bolt to the right, unlocking the door, and without turning to look at Rani, closed it shut.

She stood in the center of the bathroom, not quite understanding the previous hour's events, yet clear and centered, nonetheless. She walked over to the mirror. Despite the mascara streaks running down her cheeks, she thought she looked gorgeous. Regal, even. She balled up some toilet paper and blotted under her eyes, then splashed some cool water on her face and reapplied her lip gloss.

When she was content with her visage, Rani threw a quick glance at the *chat noir* before turning to leave the bathroom. When she opened the door, the immediate sight of the woman in royal blue startled Rani. Without saying a word, the woman smiled at Rani before entering the bathroom and locking the door.

Rani chuckled and bounced her way out of the restaurant, down Broadway, into the elevator of her office building and up to the fourteenth floor.

As the doors dinged open, she was greeted with a chorus of voices yelling, "SURPRISE! HAPPY BIRTHDAY!" Rani nearly fell over with laughter as her personal assistant placed a plastic, pink tiara on her head. Rani's secretary immediately entered with a large cake, aflame with numerous candles.

After the cheering died down, she took a breath and began blowing out the candles. When it became evident that she wouldn't be able to tackle them all on her own, she gestured to the rest of the group for their assistance.

"Thank you everyone," Rani said, tears forming once more. "Thank you for all this, but more importantly, thank you for being here. It means so much to me that you feel as passionately about this company as I do. My mission has always been to change the lives of people for the better, and I could not do that without every single one of you. So thank you. Truly, it is an honor and a pleasure."

"I know who gets the first piece of cake!" egged the CTO, handing a plate to Rani.

Rani lightly blushed at the suggestion of food.

"Um, not right now," she said. "I'm, uh, feeling pretty full after lunch. But do save me a piece!"

Rani made the rounds, personally thanking each of her employees. As they complimented her on how she looked particularly vibrant that day, she simply answered with a knowing smile.

After an hour of revelry, Rani returned to her office overlooking Madison Square Park. She dropped into her leather chair, grateful to have a moment of quiet. She scanned the ornate floral arrangements decorating the room. However, the modest clump of orange marigolds was what finally caught her eye. She plucked the card from the plastic holder and read it.

To the death. CC

She mouthed the words several times. An eerie chill enveloped her, and she stared around the room as if expecting someone to answer. Nothing responded except a soft breeze blowing through the diaphanous curtain draping the window. She recalled the moment only a few hours before when she had offered herself to death—its taste still lingering on her tongue. She opened the desk drawer and pulled out a silver-plated Zippo lighter. She flipped open the top and flicked the striker. Dangling the card over the dancing flame, Rani watched as the fire quickly engulfed the white matte paper. She then tossed it into the wastebasket, not taking her eyes off the smoldering ashes until every piece had disintegrated.

She then spied a single red rose sitting in a vase on her desk—a lone anomaly amongst the blooming bouquets. She opened the small, ivory envelope and smiled when she read the short note.

Hope it was delicious.
Ms. V.

Rani closed her eyes and leaned back, relishing the taste of the day's events. Only when her phone startled her awake twenty minutes later did she realize she'd fallen asleep.

"Ms. Greene is on the line for you," spoke the secretary over the intercom.

"Thank you. I'll take the call," Rani replied.

She pressed the button next to the red, blinking light. "Hello?"

"Happy Birthday, my love!" spoke the voice on the other end of the line.

"Thank you. It's good to hear your voice."

"Hmmmm. I've missed you all day."

"Me too. We had a sweet birthday gathering here. Did you see the *Fortune* cover?"

"I did, baby. I am so proud of you."

Rani beamed through the telephone.

"And before that? How was lunch?"

Rani stopped, then smiled before answering.

"Delicious," she replied.

"Mmmmm. I had hoped so. Can't wait to hear more tonight."

Rani paused and took a breath, calming her accelerating heart.

"So," continued the voice, "what does the birthday girl want to do this evening?"

"Well, it's been a pretty full day already. Honestly, I'd just love a quiet night at home with you."

"Your wish is my command, beautiful."

"Perfect. Oh—" Rani paused, a sly grin spreading across her face, "do you think Ms. V will make an appearance?"

"Well—that depends on if you're a good girl."

"And if I'm not a good girl?"

The voice laughed, enjoying the intrigue.

"Then she will *definitely* make an appearance."

"I love you, Veronica."

"Love you too, Rani. See you tonight."

Rani softly returned the phone to its cradle and leaned back in her chair, noticing that she still held Veronica's note in her left hand. She placed it gingerly against her full heart before losing herself in the effulgent beauty of the New York City skyline.

the nun archetype
DEVOTION, FAITH

> *This God that she worshiped consumed her. It didn't ask for a brief visit to a temple, or a small votive offering of food or coin, or a few prayers every now and then. This God wanted all of her.*
> ~ *Francine Rivers*, A Voice in the Wind

The Nun Archetype devotes her erotic energy to serving the divine. When many people hear the words "erotic" and "nun" in the same sentence, they often believe the two mix as well as oil and water. However, in remembering the original definition of eros—that is, an expression of love that connects to our fundamental creative impulse—we find that the Nun is especially capable and more than willing to surrender to her erotic power. As she makes a powerful commitment to be of service to her purpose, the Nun is the epitome of devotion.

We don't need to believe in God or become celibate to embody the Nun. All we need is a sense of faith, purpose, and passion for a cause greater than ourselves. That can look like anything from a multi-billionaire entrepreneur to a mother to an artist to a gravedigger. The Nun feels a deep connection to her spiritual life and embraces the erotic flow of her energy as "holy spirit."

In the sexual realm, the integrated Nun has a powerful connection to her sex, for it serves as the portal to her creative essence, with God as her Beloved. She also feels no shame about her genitals, as they too are an expression of the divine and can be used in the service of love.

A modern-day example of the integrated Nun is Sister Wendy Beckett, a South African-born Catholic monastic who currently resides in England. She is best known for her public television specials showcasing the history and technical skill of various artists and their creations.

When Sister Wendy speaks, every word seems to be a gourmet morsel she cannot wait to share with her viewers. It is evident how much awe, reverence, and passion she has for art. She speaks with pleasure and delight as she describes the sensual curves of the sky, fruit, women, and all manner of subjects that the artists choose to express. She does not balk in disapproval when describing the sexual ardor of nude characters depicted in paintings or sculptures. And the seemingly limitless well of wonder from which she draws is unconditional love for all of God's creations—the "dark" and the "light" both equally worthy of worship.

the shadow nun

The Nun often elicits images of a severe, cold, and angry woman hell-bent on punishing anyone who sins. However, this is an expression of the Nun's shadow, the sanctimonious Renunciate. She prioritizes spiritual pursuits and denigrates the "pleasures of the flesh." She lives in shame of her coarse human nature and seeks to rise above her own body.

The Nun's shadow goes far beyond religion. Anorexics, certain breeds of "hippies," and many "enlightenment seekers" also wrestle with the Nun's shadow. While chasing the "higher" virtues, they often cannot take care of their own worldly needs or handle physical expressions of energy, such as money, food, or possessions. In fact, they may even take pride in how much they can deny themselves, believing that contained within their suffering is the pathway to righteousness. While they may delude themselves that they are compassionate beings, they are actually caught in an ego-based struggle with their own vanity, as they belittle anyone who is not "pure" like they are.

integrated and shadow examples of the nun

- Devi: Tantric master in Daniel Odier's *Tantric Quest* who lives a secluded life in the Himalayan forest and eventually teaches him the tantric arts.
- Heloise: Twelfth century philosopher whose devotion to her beloved Abelard endures even after she takes her holy orders as a nun.
- Hestia: Greek Goddess of the hearth who does not take a partner. Known for her modest dress, inner spiritual world, and desire to live alone or in community of like-minded sisters.
- Jane Ingalls: Nun from the Netflix series, *Orange is the*

New Black. Her devotion to peace leads to her arrest after chaining herself to a flagpole near a nuclear test site.
- Pema Chödrön: American-born Buddhist nun known for her wise teachings on compassion and letting go.
- Sister Wendy Beckett: Catholic nun and art critic known for her PBS show.
- Anorexics (Renunciate Shadow).
- Religious leaders who preach fear and exclusion rather than love and inclusion (Renunciate Shadow).
- Sister Bridget: Sadistic Irish nun from *The Magdalene Sisters*, a movie based on real-life events where girls of ill repute are sent to work in a launderette (asylum) with dehumanizing conditions (Renunciate Shadow).

inviting the nun into our lives

In our sex, as in everywhere, we can cultivate the qualities of devotion and faith when we begin to think of our actions as prayer. Before making love—either alone or with a partner or partners—we can take a moment and dedicate our lovemaking to a cause beyond ourselves. Orgasm is a powerful force for manifestation. When we tap into our purpose while opening our bodies and souls to this force, it sets the stage for nothing short of miracles.

The Nun is here to teach us how to walk with humility and awe for everything on this planet. No matter how grand or trivial her work may look to others, she knows that she is in her integrity as long as she maintains her devotion to her spirit. She reminds us to bow our heads in reverence to the mysteries that influence and guide us every day. Every moment is a prayer for compassion, for she is well aware of the interconnectedness of everything. May all of us here on earth heed her invitation to dance with each other in the name of divine love.

on a sultry southern sunday

On a sultry Southern Sunday
Hazy honeysuckle in the heat
Christian soldiers fan themselves
With folded programs for relief.

The preacher, collar stained with sweat,
Says, "Turn to Psalm 23."
Daddy glances towards the acolytes
But I'm not where I should be.

I'm lyin' down in greener pastures
Inviting a quickening breath
Restoring a sad, scarred soul through
My valley of the shadow of death.

Bring those quiet waters
To a rolling, raging boil
Let my fingers do the prayin'
Anoint my head with palm oil.

Break your rod, keep your staff
Hungry hands long to feed
And your wafer-scrap holy bite
Leaves me writhing in hollow need.

And after the shepherd's spoken
The flocks, freshly blessed,

RECLAIMING EROS

Head to brunch to gorge their guilt
In feasts of righteousness.

They're born and bled to hide behind
The Good Book of the past
Tissue thin leaves won't cut their skin
When they turn the pages too fast.

But on a sultry Southern Sunday
When I'm upstairs all alone
It ain't no low-swung chariot
Comin' for to carry me home.

christina

Christina Cadorette pulled her brand new, "Tangerine Splash" hued Prius-C through the black iron gates surrounding her Malibu estate. Its bright orange color perfectly mirrored the jack o' lanterns dotting the gates of her neighbors' beachside villas, though her own home did not reflect any Halloween spirit. She'd owned the hybrid for only two days, but it already felt more familiar in her hands than the Mercedes Roadster her ex-husband gave her five years ago for her 50th birthday. The sporty, red convertible was more a gift to himself than for her—especially since she had avoided learning manual transmission during her entire driving history. Several months and three burnt clutches later, Christina figured out how to maneuver the damned thing—for the most part. But she always resented the car.

Christina saw the trade-in as a step towards her independence. She and her ex-husband, Mark, had separated nearly a year ago, but she had held on to the Roadster out of spite as they audited, appraised, sliced and diced the detritus of their twenty-five-year marriage.

"To the death!" he used to say with a devilish grin when describing their marriage—neither of them knowing how bitter that death would be.

As the gate locked behind Christina, she drove up the brick-laid path to the front door of the 9,000 square foot mansion. She depressed the emergency brake with her Stella McCartney trainer and pushed the black, round button next to the steering wheel, shutting off the car.

Her gaze shifted over the massive house—the spoils from her former life. A nominal victory given that she barely strayed from the path between her bedroom and the kitchen. The rest of the house sat untouched, like an empty, historical ghost. Five bedrooms, six-and-a-half bathrooms, a stone patio, a swimming pool, a hot tub, a fire pit, an elevator to the balconied master suite, a walk-in closet full of designer clothing and handcrafted jewelry, a game room, a media room, a dining room, a state-of-the-art kitchen, two living rooms and the infamous fireplace, all facing eighty feet of beach front property.

She recalled the fight they had over that damned fireplace. She'd always wanted one—thought there was something sumptuous and romantic about it. However, Mark thought it was absurd that a Southern California home should need a fireplace. At the time Christina couldn't understand why he had fought so hard against it. In retrospect, it was just another sideways argument playing out within their typically passive aggressive power struggles.

What began as an earnest courtship quickly devolved into a partnership based on advancing each other's social status. He was a rich and influential Hollywood lawyer. She was a beautiful model and aspiring actress. While they seemed like a power couple to outsiders, within the marriage they were strangers. Emotional intimacy had never been their modus operandi, and their marriage quickly shifted to one of static convenience. Mark fell into the role of material provider while Christina accepted her status as his trophy wife.

For the first few years of matrimony, Christina clung to the hope that things would change and that the fairy tale Mark had initially promised was on the verge of coming true. But once it became clear her fantasy would never become reality, she hid her sadness and disappointment—both in her marriage and her stalled acting career—within the world of food restriction and overexercise.

To cope with his own disappointments, Mark buried himself in work and women. So when the great fireplace battle roared between them, it felt like a breaking point into which they poured the unspoken resentments of their twenty-five-year marriage.

Exhaustion caught up with Mark first. He conceded and had the fireplace installed. The same day the installation was complete, Mark hired movers to collect nearly eighty percent of the house's contents and had them put in storage. He relocated to his Beverly Hills *pied-à-terre*—which, as one of Tinseltown's top entertainment lawyers, worked better for him anyway. It was closer to his clients and his mistresses.

Almost a year later, the barren house stood exactly the same as the day the movers left. Mark had auctioned off the majority of their estate to cover legal fees and massive alimony payments. Christina had neither the heart nor the will to refill the home to its former beauty. It suited her as its insulated hollowness mirrored her own.

The sight of Marta, the Polish housekeeper, rushing from the front door snapped Christina from her rueful nostalgia. She only kept Marta as a cleaner because Christina had a fondness for the single mother and her ten-year-old son. In truth, Christina had little need for a housekeeper—especially given that there wasn't much to clean and she had no friends to entertain anymore.

Marta's lime green cleaning garments billowed around her small frame, and her blonde bob bounced as she ran towards the Prius. Christina quickly exited the vehicle, noticing Marta's hurried approach.

"Mrs. C," Marta gasped, her thick accent barely piercing through her breathlessness.

"What is it, dear?" Christina responded, gently putting her hand on the young woman's shoulder. "Slow down. Take your time."

Marta steadied herself on the car's hood before continuing.

"It's Amadej. He was in fight in school. Broke nose and arm. He is in hospital now. I must to go get. I am sorry. I am not done with house."

"Of course, dear. Do not worry," Christina soothed. "Take care of your son, and take as much time off as you need."

"Thank you, Mrs. C." Marta quickly turned towards the red Nissan sedan parked next to the Prius.

"Oh!" Marta cried, facing Christina once more. "There was noise in basement while I clean. I go down. Maybe hungry animals looking for scraps? Anyway, I find nothing, but I notice box all bite up, so I bring upstairs. It is in kitchen now. Sorry I not put away."

Christina paused. A box? She didn't know anything else was left after Mark's exodus.

"It's no problem. There's no need to apologize," said Christina, hoping to mollify the harried housekeeper.

Marta nodded her head sharply and pursed her lips into a tight smile before jumping into her car and speeding off.

Continuing her routine, Christina walked around to the back of her car, opened the hatchback, pulled out her fluorescent orange gym bag and headed for the oak front door. She had just completed forty-five minutes of spinning followed by an hour with a personal trainer. Now that Christina was home, she anticipated her usual lunch: one twelve-ounce can of Diet Coke, one egg fried in a two-second shot of Pam cooking spray and one cup of steamed broccoli drizzled with two teaspoons of balsamic vinegar. Because her yoga teacher was coming for a lesson later in the afternoon, she would allow herself two squares of raw dark chocolate as "dessert."

Christina stepped into the foyer and dropped her bag by the entrance. Heading to the kitchen to begin her feeding ritual, she stopped when she saw the gnawed cardboard box by the stove. It looked as if it had spent years rotting in moisture. Black, moldy dots marbled the bottom edges.

She pulled the top flap open. The damp cardboard nearly disintegrated in her hands. She wondered how Marta hauled the whole thing upstairs in one piece. Gingerly, Christina peeled back the other flaps, revealing four stacks of books. Miraculously, they had remained mostly dry—excepting the edges in direct contact with the moist cardboard; those were warped.

Christina's discovery instantly transported her to a bygone era—a coming-of-age fairy tale full of hope and promise. On top lay two photo albums with family pictures slipping out from their formerly adhesive pages. Before clumsily dropping the cumbersome pile on the floor, she caught a peek of her teenage-self holding Little James, her baby brother—the photo taken only a few years before she would abandon her monotonous Kansas childhood for the golden promised land of California. She felt a twinge of guilt as she recalled her bi-annual ritual of tossing her brother's Christmas cards and birthday notes in the trash unopened.

Underneath the old photo album rested a professional look book packed with headshots and modeling tear sheets featuring "Christina Anderson"—a souvenir from her early days in the industry. Christina flipped through the pages, marveling at how important each of those photos was to her thirty years ago—and how insignificant they seemed now. The gap between her optimistic memories and her current numbness formed an aching bubble in the center of her chest. She snapped the leather-bound time capsule shut and tossed it to the side, unable to bear any more.

Fortunately for her swelling emotions, the rest of the box's contents belonged to Mark. Old textbooks from law school were piled on top of one another, each showing various degrees of wear and tear. Some had worn-out spines, while others looked nearly brand new, were it not for the water damage.

Christina continued to dig through the musty tomes until she discovered two small paperbacks that were out of place amongst the technical publications. One was a copy of Kate Chopin's *The Awakening*. Christina remembered reading the book as a junior in high school but couldn't recall most of the story's details—only the heroine's adultery and self-inflicted demise.

The second was a book of poetry from an author she didn't recognize. Skimming the biography printed on the back, Christina discovered the collection represented the complete works of Sarah Ann McDonald, an African-American Southern woman whose work spanned the '50s and '60s. Though married for most of her adult life, the obscure poet was a closeted lesbian and had killed herself upon reaching middle age in the early 1970s—just months after giving birth to her only child, Matthew.

But what caught Christina's attention was the cursive inscription penned in both books:

June 1972
To my darling M,
Please remember me with fondness and love, as I do you.
Forgive me.
S

"S?"

1972. Mark was a pre-teen then, living in Greenwich, CT with the rest of the Cadorette clan. Perhaps it was an old girlfriend?

"Morbid present to give to a beau," Christina silently mused.

She stared at the delicate writing, hoping some clue would pop out from the author's blue ink. The colors blurred before her eyes—her attention softening—until her memory startled her upright. His older sister. Mark kept tightlipped about her, never divulging any details of her adolescent passing. And since both of Mark's elderly parents passed shortly before Christina and Mark married, she never had the opportunity to ask anyone else about her death.

An eerie chill coursed from the fringes of the page through her fingertips. She glanced around the room as her thinning, bleached hair prickled along her scalp. Given the inauspicious fates of the women within the pages, Christina wondered if his sister's gifts were covert suicide notes.

Though stricken with sickening horror, she began flipping through the deceased poet's folio. The words bled together into one gray stream until she landed on a black-and-white sketch. Faded with age, it seemed to be the outline of a young girl staring through a church window. The figure's thin bones protruded from her bloodless skin. A garland of marigolds perched on her disheveled hair—the decaying flowers tumbling over her dirty ears.

Christina noticed a poem on the opposite page, which corresponded to the illustration, and began reading.

OUT

I never came.
Out.

I have always been.
Out.

Glimpsing the memory of a warm den,
Your devout hands clasped over the fire,
Browned, braided bread steams
As your wet lips part to give the blessing.

But I, staring at the pickins
Of something that reminds me of love,
Cannot reach across the twisted divide
To touch the remembrance of you,

Even though your aproned skirt,
Dusted in fresh white flour,
Sits just around the nicked bend
Of our hardwood table.

I watch you recite prayers,
While I stare from behind
A pane of colored glass painted by the
Winter fog of my shaky breath.

RECLAIMING EROS

Patiently I wait for invitation,
While spring rains sting my tear-stained face
(I bet you'd feel it on that cold shoulder
If you stepped out here once in a while).

On the summer porch I silently quiver,
Shrouding myself, despite the heat,
And heeding the words you spoke
After my first trans-gression:

"Don't let anyone see you like that."

Locking my mouth, I dutifully obey
And tuck my tail between my legs,
As ravenous winds whirl autumn leaves
Around my starving bones.

From the moment I was born
I've stood outside the lines of convention
And donned the garb of seasonal Queens
Beheaded for their dissension.

But though I've lived a life beyond
The tender graze of your fingertips,
Never once did I feign my angular truth
With a rounded lie.

And even when you looked right through me
With your gaze of convenient invisibility,
I've always been. Right. Out. Here.
Waiting for you to never see me.

No.

I never came.
Out.

I have always been.
Out.

And I thank God for that,
For these cave walls have now liberated me,
While yours keep you locked inside
Frightened of your shadow, eternally.

    She read the poem twice more, the words piercing her carefully constructed shell. She thought about the "rounded lie" of a life she'd been living—eternally frightened of her own shadow. She thought of the years she'd wasted starving herself, silently screaming for help—all the while knowing Mark would never see her. Finally realizing she had been holding her breath, Christina lifted her glazed eyes towards the ceiling and forcefully exhaled while the book slipped from her fingers and dropped onto the white, tiled floor. Sick with nausea, she ran down the hall to the half-bath near the front door and threw herself at the base of the toilet. Dry heaves wracked her skeletal frame, but nothing came up.

After a few moments, she leaned against the wall, exhausted. Emptiness cinched her like an iron corset—the weight of her own unhappiness paralyzing her.

"What have I been doing to myself all these years? Who have I become?" Christina silently questioned. Fighting the heaviness in her body, she grabbed the counter and hoisted herself up to face the mirror over the sink. Despite the makeup and plastic surgery, Christina looked ungracefully old. The mascara, the rouge, the eyelift, the botox, the lip injections—nothing could conceal years of self-loathing and despair.

Forcefully, she yanked the hot water lever and splashed her face. She scraped and scrubbed herself raw, desperate to expose the woman buried beneath the surface. Without drying her skin, she turned off the faucet, opened her eyes and peeled the tank top off her emaciated figure. She stared at the woman-thing reflecting back at her.

As ravenous winds whirl autumn leaves
Around my starving bones.

She hesitantly placed her hands just above her hair as if expecting to discover marigolds crowning her. Numbly, she traced her fingers over her waxy face and down to the crêpe-like skin of her throat before stopping at her implanted breasts. Her nipples jutted like rocks under her touch. She skimmed her hands over her protruding ribs, an echo of pride and disbelief swelling within her as she recalled the arduous years she'd spent maintaining her cadaverous figure. She placed her palms over her concave belly—her greatest fear and foe. Christina had learned how to quiet her hunger ages ago, but that conquest seemed trifling compared to the emptiness that now consumed her.

The photographs from her youth flashed before her—their haunting figments bearing no resemblance to the ghost in the mirror. In light of these realizations, all she felt was pressing coldness.

Slowly, Christina backed out of the bathroom and turned to face the main room, taking in her surroundings. She could make out the darkened rectangles tracing the walls—staining leftover from antique frames where important paintings once hung. Despite the house's vacuity, it was still an impressive structure. Massive columns ran from the first floor all the way to the three-storied ceiling. The clear-blue water and colorful gardens peeked through the glass doors on her right.

"How could a woman with so much feel so little?" she wondered. Christina shivered with cold. Though the thermometer read seventy-eight degrees, the chill instigated her desire for warmth.

Without thinking, she climbed the stairs to the third floor, gripping the railing the entire way. At the top of the staircase, she steadied herself and ambled towards the door at the end of the hall. Hurrying through the master bedroom, she decisively entered the bathroom and closed the door behind her.

She walked to the sink and rummaged through the cabinet. Bath salts, gels, lotions and perfumes sat clustered together—the forgotten remnants of half-hearted holiday gifts obviously given to her as a last resort for "the woman who has everything." Christina never thought much of those trinkets but was now grateful for her acquaintances' thoughtfulness. She grabbed the glass jar closest to her and headed to the tub. Squinting her eyes, she debated which of the multiple knobs dispensed hot water—as she was used to quickly showering in the stall opposite the bath. Unable to mentally process the jigsaw of dials, she took a chance on the one furthest to the left. Within seconds, steaming water flowed from the gold faucet. Christina shook the pale purple salts into the tub. The smell of lavender filled the room.

She slid off her yoga pants and stood in the middle of the porcelain basin, the scalding water rising over her ankles. Adjusting to the prickling heat, she slowly sat down and leaned against the tub's sloped edge. Her skin luxuriated in the wet warmth. As the rushing water splashed at her feet, Christina closed her eyes. The forceful sound of the faucet's waterfall reverberated throughout the room, muffling any other noise.

Letting go of sight and sound opened a vacuum in her mind. Her constricted body yielded within her mental spaciousness. To her surprise, the space between her thighs softened and pulsed in a way she thought she'd lost due to the ravages of age and lack of marital fulfillment. In that moment, hidden within the pockets of remembrance, emerged an apparition of yesteryear.

A girl, no more than thirteen years old, took shape in the center of the room. She recognized the fresh innocence in the young girl's face as the expression Christina once wore. The figure sported a pair of simple Levi's and a T-shirt, her budding breasts barely hidden beneath the thin, white cotton. Her unkempt, brown hair fell down to her waist.

What captured Christina's attention was the way the girl raised her arms in devoted reverie, as if receiving a divine transmission. An angelic glow engulfed the child. Christina recalled a time when she too was devoted to God. In the early years of her adolescence, she had attended church faithfully and had pledged her life in service to Jesus. On the weekends, she worked at homeless shelters, hoping to alleviate the suffering of God's children. She visited nursing homes to keep the elderly company, playing her guitar and singing hymns.

On Wednesday nights, she babysat the young kids, while the adults attended service. She looked forward to Vacation Bible School every summer and was overjoyed when she was old enough to attend the church's summer retreat with the other teenagers. It was there Christina had had her first awakening; the memory of that moment formed around the specter of the young girl.

One hot summer afternoon, the youth leaders called everyone in for a worship service. Drum beats, guitar chords and young voices charismatically sang Christian folk songs, which greeted the teens as they entered. Christina stood near the instruments, drinking in their sonic praise. Like most everyone else, she turned her palms to the sky and closed her eyes. Suddenly, everything slipped to a fuzzy black. The next thing Christina knew, the musicians were standing over her, concerned looks on their faces, and her head was wedged between the bottom of a music stand and the bass drum. Though she didn't remember the sequence of events that knocked her horizontal, Christina recalled a sense of lightness and clarity. She laughed as the young parishioners frantically buzzed about her.

Was she hurt?
Did she trip?
Did the devil get her?

"No," she internally confirmed—she was not hurt. What she was, though, was free. A giggle surfaced to young Christina's lips as the warmth of love held her. In all her years in the church, she had never touched God as directly as in that moment. She thought back to the times she'd spoken in tongues, gotten "slain in the spirit" or received exorcist healings. Compared to the genuine freedom she had found laid out on the floor, those other experiences seemed phony—like hysterical acts born out of an unspoken complicity between herself and the church leaders, each seeking their own form of attention and validation.

Over the months following her fall, she'd begun to notice more of the counterfeits and manipulations of her beloved community: book burnings, certain music deemed "sinful," the absurd demand that each of the girls remain a virgin and an increased call for separation from the rest of society. Christina was all for Jesus, but she couldn't reconcile the church's beliefs with her own deeper understanding of the love of Christ. Her disenchantment grew until she left spirituality altogether, declaring herself a staunch rationalist.

The sound of water splashing on the tile floor interrupted Christina's musings. She jumped when she noticed the overflow and quickly reached to turn off the faucet. Determining that the deluge had done little damage, she leaned back in the tub once more.

Without thinking, her hands went to her thighs, normally the most hated part of her body. She squeezed them but without the normal disgust and dread. She felt the softness and sagging frailty of a body nearly whittled out of existence. She then moved her hands to her sunken belly—patched and pulled and stretched and trimmed. She'd spent egregious amounts of money on bodily perfection in the hopes that one day someone would tell her she was finally worthy of love.

Realizing there was no love to be found in her futile efforts, Christina's blood flooded with hatred—chilling her veins and puckering her skin, despite the scalding water. Hatred for life. Hatred for her absent father. Hatred for her cold mother. Hatred for her jealous stepfather. Hatred for society's obsession with appearance. Hatred for doctors who make their living cutting insecure women. Hatred for every man who had ever told her how she would be perfect if she could just get that *one* thing fixed, removed, tightened, augmented or adjusted.

But mostly, the hatred burned for her self—for believing their lies. For losing faith in her own power. For choosing resignation over magic.

She slid her fingers over the slippery folds of her pussy. A waking fire flickered inside her hibernating body. Something akin to hunger but more unrelenting—a voracity emanating from a forgotten void that demanded her obeisance. It felt like an act of rebellion—daring to stir her forgotten flesh in rejection of remaining frozen.

Though tentative, Christina followed the guiding force humming through her fingertips. Exploring, she skimmed over the hardening bump of her clit and moved down towards the bottom of her opening, taking in the alternating slick and coarse texture.

In all her years searching for physical perfection, she'd never lasered her bikini line. That day, she was grateful for that decision, for now her hair felt like an extension of her skin, each caress shimmering up to her belly.

Christina continued to stroke, light and feathery. The tickling spark gave way to a growing fire that blazed over her cunt and ass. The thick steam hovering over the bathwater seeped into her skin. Sweat formed above her mouth and trickled down her lips. She involuntarily extended her tongue to catch the salty drops.

Suddenly, the young girl appeared again, but this time two older teenage boys flanked her, one of them holding a swaddled baby. Her brothers. Seeing the twins and Little James unlocked a dark chasm lodged deep within her heart. The heat traveled up her fingertips, over her navel, between her breasts and landed square in the center of her chest. The pain of lost years bubbled within her. She imagined their anger over her chosen estrangement. But in their innocent eyes, she saw nothing but love. A sweet ache overtook her as the first orgasmic swell crested and the figures faded into the air.

Then her mother, father and stepfather materialized next to her younger self. An uncomfortable queasiness rolled through her stomach. Her parents' presence in juxtaposition to such a private moment felt embarrassing. But when Christina slowed down and looked at them, they ceased being "mom and dad and Bernie," and she simply saw three human beings with all their wondrous faults and glories. As the next peak overtook her, her compassion flooded and engulfed the apparitions, until they too were no more.

Lastly she saw Mark. Her distant and dispassionate memory of him instantly transformed into sweet longing. Through the faded hair and wrinkled forehead, Christina remembered the gallant, young man who'd promised her the world on their first date. The fact that he'd failed his mission seemed irrelevant. In fact, it had always been an impossible task. Christina understood that now. The world was not for him to give—it was for her to experience.

The figure moved closer, each step pushing Christina higher towards the widening apex. He brought his face directly before hers. She closed her eyes, too frightened to behold him so closely. But at the final reach, she flashed them open and not only saw his face, but also her own, her parents, brothers, friends, enemies—even people she had never met. The faces before her reflected her own—and hers was the face of God.

Her throat split through the calcified cotton of unexpressed desire, and she screamed as her body merged with something that could only be described as "Oneness." Pockets of rigidity gave way to unbearable pleasure. The endless tidal wave of orgasm rushed through her, though she remained transfixed in stillness.

Finally, she fell limp—offering herself to death. The scent of marigolds, raw milk and burnt flesh filled her nose. The light, the blackening light that had blighted her all those years ago, was there again—only now, she was big enough to hold it and wise enough to recognize it as God's Grace.

Christina sensed she was collecting herself once more when she felt the murky water cooling on her skin, though she continued to sit still for several minutes. She slowly brought her hands up and rubbed her face, smearing the floral tang of salt and lavender on her lips. The taste of rebirth.

She grabbed the edges of the tub, hoisted herself up and reached for the white towel, monogrammed in gold with the letters 'CC.' She stepped out onto the plush mat and whisked away the water beads. Dropping the towel, she made her way over to the line of hooks near the door. Christina shakily grabbed her orange robe and wrapped it around her before carefully stepping into the bedroom and collapsing onto the bed. The folds of the feather quilt puffed upwards as she landed and the unsashed robe opened, spilling forth her breasts and belly.

Christina welcomed the fresh air on her hot skin. She clutched her torso and trembled as thick tears threatened to cascade over her eyelids. She had once again merged with the burning hands of the Holy Spirit, just as she had done when she was thirteen, only to find herself abandoned once more.

"Help me!"

Christina cried, grief rattling through her.

"Help me, please."

Her prayer gave way to jangled sobbing. She placed both her hands on her heart, trying to keep her rib cage from shattering as her heart hammered relentlessly in her chest.

Suddenly she realized that what she was feeling was not grief, but unbearable, heart-shattering love. Indescribable love that rests on the tip of the tongue. The kind of love that clangs and bangs within the heart, yet never finds its way out of the restrictive confines of the flesh. It was the kind of love only God understands and most humans spend eternities trying to purchase.

Breathing deeply, Christina surrendered into the widening space created by this newfound love. She felt the terry cloth nestling the back of her body—the first time she had noticed its softness. She instantly fell in love with the fabric. As strange as that would seem in retrospect, it made perfect sense to her in the moment.

Christina saw the sun's angular rays streaming from the window, highlighting the tiny bits of dust dancing in the light.

She fell in love with them, too. As she sat up, she discovered the beauty in *everything* and was shocked at the years she'd spent *not* loving it all.

"Thank you," Christina whispered. "Thank you."

Awash in tranquil bliss, she gently rolled off the bed and onto her feet. Transcendent lightness carried her to the large closet, where she crouched before a massive line of shoes. She reached behind them and procured a tiny, wooden jewelry box. It looked worn and provincial compared to the others bejeweled in opulence. But its quiet modesty comforted her. Like coming home.

Besides the two photo albums, that box was the only souvenir from her youth—the only trinket Christina carried into exile. Tenderly lifting the lid, she saw a collection of papers, notes and cards. She sifted through the papers, hit the felted bottom and fumbled around until she found a small sliver of metal. Pulling it out she held it in her tiny hands, admiring its simplicity. Her great-grandmother's silver cross. It had quite a bit of tarnish on it, but that didn't diminish its impact. She loved it in that moment as much as she had loved it when her meemaw first gave it to her.

Standing up, Christina softly stepped towards the bathroom and found a container of silver cleaner. She dunked the pendant and chain in the chemical solution and waited a bit, watching the years of neglect disappear. After a few minutes, she rinsed it with water and patted it dry. She then placed the chain around her neck, hooked the clasp and adjusted the cross so it rested just below the center of her throat.

Looking in the mirror, she noticed how perfectly it sat upon her skin—as if it had never spent forty years at the bottom of a box. She brushed her fingertips against the pendant's sparkling edges, admiring her complexion underneath the cool metal. She gazed up at her face and smiled—something she had not done for quite some time.

Suddenly her belly rumbled. It was a sound Christina had nearly forgotten after years of self-imposed famine. Her mind clenched for a moment, racing through her mental inventory of caloric intake and pantry items. The oatmeal, stevia and coffee she had allowed herself for breakfast. The fried egg and broccoli she had planned (but had forgotten to eat) for lunch. The can of tuna and salad greens for dinner.

Yet, the more she thought about what she wanted within the confines of her prescribed regimen, the more exhausted she felt. She didn't have it in her anymore to be a slave to misery. She was now a devoted servant to her own heart.

Christina turned and walked out of the bedroom. Gathering her robe around her, she headed down the stairs and into the kitchen. Before habit could hijack her intentions, she texted her yoga teacher, canceling the day's session. As she set down the phone, she spied the small painting of marigolds hanging by the refrigerator—a wedding gift from one of Mark's early clients. A smile curled on her lips as she opened the miscellaneous drawer and pulled out the card of the florist she used when Mark was at his New York City office. She dialed the number and held her breath as the line rang.

"Hello, Gramercy Florist. How may I help you?"

"Yes, hello? I'd like to send some flowers to someone. Please have them delivered by tomorrow."

"OK. What kind of bouquet would you like?"

"Marigolds," she said, staring at the painting.

"What else?"

"That's it."

"Just marigolds?" asked the florist, surprised at the simplicity of the order.

"Yes. And write 'To the death' on the card."

"Should I note who it's from?" asked the florist incredulously.

"The initials 'CC' will do."

"Address?"

Christina hesitated. She hadn't needed Mark's east coast address for some time, and she'd deleted all of his contact info once the divorce was finalized.

"Uhhh," she stalled, scanning the rolodex of her long-term memory.

"22 East 23 Street. Suite 1404," she finally blurted. She figured either it was right and Mark would receive the flowers, or it was wrong and someone would get exactly the medicine they needed.

"To whom is this addressed?"

"Leave that blank," said Christina, smiling. She wrapped up the order, giving the florist her credit card info. When she finished, she placed her iPhone down with a satisfied plop.

She opened Marta's pantry, where the housekeeper usually kept some food for her son when he wasn't in school.

Christina found a fresh loaf of whole wheat bread, a container of organic peanut butter and a jar of raw, local honey. Her mouth watered. Making a mental note to replace Marta's groceries, she pulled out the bread and placed two slices in the toaster. A warm, caramel scent filled the kitchen. She grabbed the honey and peanut butter and placed them on the counter. She wanted to keep moving and give no pause to the prospect of turning back.

She found a plate and two knives in the dishwasher. The moment she set them down, the bread jumped from the toaster. Gingerly taking the hot toast between her fingertips, she dropped them onto the plate. Then, opening the jar of peanut butter, she plunged in the knife and spread the oily paste onto one of the slices in an oozy smear. Placing the knife between her lips, she licked its delicious remnants. The rich, nutty flavor melted on her tongue. She did the same with the honey, spreading and tasting its bright, golden sweetness.

She pressed the two pieces together and walked out onto the back patio. The bright view of a late afternoon in Malibu greeted her eyes. She sat on the edge of the wooden steps that wound down to the beach. Looking at the object in her hands, she marveled at how such a tiny thing had held so much power over her. She closed her eyes and inhaled, taking in the scent of warm bread and salty air.

Finally, Christina placed the crust in her mouth, tore off a bit and slowly chewed. Each bite required courage—and yet it also reminded her of her strength. Christina ate until there was nothing left but victory and relief.

Lounging back on the wooden deck, she opened her robe, revealing her naked body to the azure sky, and placed her hands on her belly. She couldn't recall the last time she felt so free and so full. She closed her eyes for a moment. Then, without thinking, Christina jumped up and ran naked into the ocean, screaming with rebellious delight. The chilly October water initially shocked her bare skin, but she continued to swim until the cold felt like a tingling embrace. Minutes passed as twilight began to dance upon the waves around her. When she noticed the moon rising above the horizon, Christina nodded her head towards the shimmering orb in a silent gesture of reverence. Then she turned to face the shore, paddled towards the darkening sands and made her way back home.

the mother archetype
CREATION, WISDOM

> *A man is a great thing upon the earth, and through eternity—but every jot of the greatness of man is unfolded out of woman,*
> *First the man is shaped in the woman, he can then be shaped in himself.*
> ~ Walt Whitman, "Unfolded Out of the Folds,"
> Leaves of Grass

While the Whore is often the most misunderstood of all the archetypes, the Mother may be both the most revered *and* reviled due to the direct, personal experience most people have with her. Everyone has a mother; however, many people often have troubling experiences with mothers—either through emotional and/or physical abandonment or smothering (more on that in the Shadow section). Therefore, many people can spend lifetimes searching for feminine companionship, not realizing that the love and nurturance they seek is the unacknowledged mother within themselves. When the external mother is forgiven, we can then forgive the mother within and walk into relationships with a sense of gratitude, connection, and fullness, rather than trying to feed our perceived lack from an outside source. This is the hallmark of spiritual maturation—to learn to parent oneself.

The Mother not only gives birth to biological children, she also facilitates the gestation of art, ideas, companies, and any form of self-expression. She nurtures other forms of life, even if they do not come directly from her body. We often see this in hospital caretakers, nannies, environmentalists (protecting "Mother Earth"), and managers within a corporation.

If one feminine archetype were to encompass the essence of all the others, the Mother would be it. We find within her many aspects of the previous archetypes: the ability to forgive her children and see them through fresh eyes (Virgin); her capacity to hold space and set boundaries (Whore); her fierce protectiveness (Warrior); her ability to wield social power effectively (Queen); and her sacrifice and service to the divine (Nun). Additionally, one subtype of the Mother—the Grandmother—includes both the fertility of the Mother as well as the wisdom of the Crone, a wise elder who no longer has the power to physically give birth.

It is this wisdom that gives the Mother her capacity for destruction—the balancing counterpart to her power of creation. As each moment is born, the old one must pass away, and it is through a Mother's wisdom that she discerns what can stay and what must be released. The Hindu Goddess Kali Ma—also referenced in the Warrior—is one such Mother/Destroyer. A cultural example is a Mother who sees through her children's dishonesty and destroys that illusion to teach them truth.

Another place we find the Mother/Destroyer is in the jungles of Peru, where the ancient, medicinal vine, ayahuasca, grows and is still consumed in sacred ceremonies. Known as "the vine of death" or "the vine of the soul," ayahuasca is believed by shamans to house the "Grandmother spirit." By imbibing ayahuasca, some people report receiving messages from the Grandmother spirit and experiencing profound spiritual awakening. However, they might also endure extreme physical and mental pain, such as intense purging, feelings of going crazy, or a sense of being on the brink of death. In these descriptions, one sees the wise yet destructive Mother/Destroyer burning away what is false so that her children may be reborn into clarity and freedom. "A farewell to my shadow is not my death; it's my rebirth in darkness," offers poet Munia Khan. This statement perfectly encapsulates the essence of the Mother/Destroyer—for with her sternness comes great love.

The Mother is the feminine counterpart to the masculine "Father"—for it is through them *both* that life is created. While the Father plants the seeds, the Mother houses within her body the nourishment to sustain and birth all of existence. Neither the Mother nor the Father lives without the other, and in fact, both are housed within the embodiment of motherhood—a tenet exemplified through the East Asian deity, Quan Yin.

Although usually associated with Buddhism, Quan Yin's legend permeates many religions in countries including China, Japan, Korea, Thailand, Vietnam, and Nepal. Her story and iconography shift between cultures: some depict her as masculine, some as feminine, some as androgynous, some as transitioning from masculine to feminine, and some as hermaphroditic. Yet throughout them all, Quan Yin is consistently portrayed as a compassionate mother-goddess of mercy and unconditional love—analogous to the Mother Mary figure in Christian mythology.

the shadow mother

Because the Mother has many faces, she also possesses several shadow aspects. For our purposes, we will focus on internal and external expressions of the Mother shadow. Internally speaking, if all of her nurturing is focused inward, she represents the Absent Mother. She may selfishly pour her energy into a career or relationship and not attend to the needs of her children. She is often great at birthing children or ideas but has very little grounding to nurture them to fruition. She may loathe her children and remain cold and distant, withholding love as a punishment for the crime of their being born.

Conversely, if a Mother involves herself too much in her children's lives, she may end up devouring them by using her children to satisfy all her unmet needs. The stereotype of the mother guilt-tripping her kids who don't visit is a prime example of what Caroline Myss deems, "The Devouring Mother"[32]—an external expression of the Mother shadow. This is a woman whose emotional nourishment and wellbeing depends upon the attention of her children. Because they

---

[32] Myss, 401.

never had the chance to individuate from the mother, they are always enmeshed with her. Unless the children learn to support themselves and grow into fully expressed humans, the Devouring Mother will destroy any part of her children that does not directly reflect her own vision of how they should be. Everything in their world is about her, she believes, making her the consummate narcissist.

Another externalized Mother shadow is the Overly Devoted Mother. She will do *anything* for the sake of her children, even to the point of her own starvation. This piece also contains the Nun's shadow in that she will deny her physical, emotional, and psychological needs for the supposed greater good of her children's growth. A cultural example is the soccer mom who runs around town giving her children everything that they want, while she suffers in silence from mental and physical maladies. This woman gives from an empty well, erroneously equating being a "good mother" with "martyrdom." She is similar to the Devouring Mother in that her emotional needs come from her children, except the one who is devoured is herself.

integrated and shadow examples of the mother

- Ajima: Word meaning "grandmother," these were Nepalese goddesses who were highly revered and represented the female ancestors of the Newar people.
- Boldogasszony: Hungary's figure of the Virgin Mother; ancient Magyar goddess of birth, fertility, and harvest.

- Kali Ma: Mother/Destroyer figure in Hindu mythology.
- Mawu: Dahomey (former kingdom now in present-day Benin) creator goddess, who combined with her twin brother-husband, Lisa, to transform into an androgynous or two-spirited deity.
- Melania: Known as one of the "desert mothers," she was an early Christian leader who used her wealth and rank to care for Christian prisoners; she gave birth to monastic life in the desert.
- Mother Mary: Ultimate expression of motherhood in Christian mythology. Marigolds are named in honor of her (Mary's gold) potentially in reference to early poverty-stricken Christians who placed the flowers at her feet as an offering when they could not afford gold. Marigolds are also sometimes referred to as the "flower of grief," perhaps as a reference to the grief Mother Mary felt when Jesus died. Marigolds as a symbol of death and the Mother/Destroyer appear in Mexican Día de los Muertos celebrations as well as Hindu rituals as a symbol of surrender.
- Oshun: Deity of the Yoruba people in Southern Nigeria. She is generally thought of as the nurturer of humanity. Goddess of Water. Mother of birds and fishes.
- Quan Yin: Mother figure in Asian cultures that symbolizes compassion. She is often depicted as a variety of genders.
- Amanda: Tom and Laura's mother from Tennessee Williams' *The Glass Menagerie* (Devouring Mother

Shadow).
- Livia Soprano: Tony Soprano's mother from *The Sopranos*, played by Nancy Marchand, who is emotionally cold and unsupportive but still uses guilt-based tactics to manipulate her son (Absent & Devouring Mother Shadow).
- Petunia Dursley from the *Harry Potter* book series: Harry's aunt who thinks her imbecilic son, Dudley, can do no wrong (Overly Devoted Mother Shadow).

inviting the mother into our lives

The Mother's capacity for creation and destruction comes from her ability to balance the energies of both masculine and feminine. She transcends gender into a unique expression of Oneness. One practice we can use to tap into the Mother's power in the sexual arena involves the breath. Sitting while facing a partner, we can inhale as our partner exhales, then exhale while our partner inhales. If practiced alone, we can imagine the earth exhaling into us as we breathe in nourishment, and then returning that nourishment to the earth as we exhale. This practice can happen before the clothes come off or in the middle of an orgasmic peak. The balance between inhalation and exhalation (creation and destruction) can put us into a heightened state of awareness and increase our capacity to experience our bodies, our partners' bodies, and our erotic energy.

The Mother invites us to seek balance between when we nurture ourselves and nurture others. She also teaches us when it is time to give birth to new ideas (creation) and when it is time to let go of that which no longer serves (destruction). She asks us to tap into her wisdom through connection with the earth and with our own creativity. Her compassion extends from gentle kindness to fierce protection. The Mother is the ultimate expression of the feminine's capacity to bring life into the world. By surrendering to her wisdom, we have the opportunity to heal the divide between all genders—for it is through their union that we finally touch the life-giving Oneness of eros.

great mother

Seven logs form a circle.
Fallen sisters,
Earthbound Pleiades,
Where life feeds upon death.

A thundering orifice,
The matriarchal maw,
Swallows the night
And opens the portal

Where newborns arise
Upon the heels
Of those descending
Via Charon's water-hearse.

Even in death
Her fallen trees don't stop giving
And continue to do so
Long after our own flesh wakes no more.

Fresh soil is piled upon
Layers of sedimentary tombs
As martyred wood chips
Dot the earth.

We walk upon
This timber corpse,

CANDICE DAWN

A portent of
Our own end of days.

Ancestral apparitions
And medicine ghosts
Dance between
Her wooden thighs.

We sit upon these pointed stumps
Like greedy babies
Drinking the sap-milk
Of her hardened breasts.

The Great Mother's naked body
Lies before us
In the mottled bark
Of arboreal decay.

nnenne

Staring out from her living room window, Nan gazed upon the neighbors' stained-glass oriel located on the fourth story of their Tudor-style home. She envisioned herself in their attic with the sun casting prisms upon her naked body as the light passed through the colored panes. She would gather her strength and, in one determined leap, smash her way through the glass kaleidoscope. On the concrete below, her broken body would peacefully lie surrounded by blood and rainbow shards glinting in the sunlight.

This was a common late afternoon daydream. She thought about death. Often. Audre Lorde. Toni Morrison. Alice Walker. May Ayim. On the surface these were individuals working against a system that knew not how to hold the force known as "woman." But to her, they were more than that: they were poets surrendered to their own rhythm—having chosen their own fates with a definitive period rather than a lingering question mark.

She intimately knew this dark iambic two-step, having taken a bottle of painkillers one month after her daughter was born forty-three years ago. The postpartum depression, coupled with her twin sister's suicide the very same week of Ella's birth, was the only time the morbid dance threatened to overtake her.

But she survived. And though the impulse to rush towards her impending epilogue certainly still lingered, the pen had yet to lay its final marks upon her wrinkled parchment. Perhaps "conscience does make cowards of us all," she thought, eyeing Shakespeare's First Folio—presented to her upon her retirement from teaching.

Despite her constant musings, she did not romanticize death. She had hoped at seventy-five she would have already come to terms with that "natural" part of life, but instead she grew more petrified as the years went on. She only had her poets to fill the void of her mortal procrastination—echoing their wisdom through languaged rays that shrouded her as one whose life depended upon verbal apricity.

Unconsciously, she ambled towards the bookshelf where her framed degree from Spelman was perched—an appropriate location for a nostalgic English major. Maybe it was the arctic cold snap, the long darkness of that evening's Winter Solstice or the many Christmas and Hanukkah cards she had just signed that caused an unusual heaviness to weigh on Nan. Using the bookshelf for support, she slowly ran her fingers over the tomes of literary mothers long departed—their cracked spines revealing years of intimate companionship. She started to pick one up but quickly slipped it back into place when she heard a familiar jangling at the front door.

Daniel silently swore as he wrestled his keys from the notoriously stubborn lock. The aperture's unwillingness to release its tenacious grip upon the grooved metal provided a frustrating power struggle every time he returned home. It had gotten worse over time. The dance between Atlanta's formidable heat and humidity (an annual visitor demanding entry into every crevice of the city) and the city's unshakeable winter frost (predictably surprising to even the most seasoned of Southerners) had swollen and contracted the brass beyond functioning, like an overplayed accordion. Though it had been years since the latch had started to falter, he'd never gotten around to replacing it.

"Goddamnit!" he cursed, nearly ripping the knob from its bore.

"Be careful there, hun," Nan said, smiling. "You'll blow a stent. Or two."

It had been a year since the dizziness and pain began but only three months since his procedure. Though he came out just fine—and had more energy these days—his brush with mortality shook him up more than he wanted to admit. They were only recently allowed to joke about it. Or so she thought.

"You're not helping, Nan. One of these days I'm gonna get trapped outside this house," he muttered, quickly tapping the mezuzah and kissing his fingers before tossing the keys with a bit more force than usual on the foyer table. Without closing the front door, he brushed past the menorah-topped Christmas tree and headed straight for his office—more specifically, the scotch. He gripped the glass as if he were punishing it for its unmalleability and haphazardly poured the amber liquid, concerned less about filling the vessel and more about expressing his furious need for the drink.

"Tough meeting?" she asked.

"Yeah. Something like that," he muttered.

Nan watched as he sharply turned the ignition lever for the gas fireplace and sank into his leather chair. He stared blankly at the massive patchwork of books that dotted the shelves.

Everything from Homer to Jonathan Safran Foer squeezed itself into those rectangular spaces—lifetimes of knowledge that offered him no comfort in the moment.

Nan shifted her eyes to the framed wedding photo on Daniel's desk. The year was 1967—only a few months after the Supreme Court legalized interracial marriage in Loving v. Virginia. Nan wore a modest lace gown she'd sewn herself. Daniel donned a white pantsuit with a frilly peach shirt. They both had marigolds tucked behind their ears.

Daniel's wedding garb was the same attire he'd worn five years earlier when he took Nan on their first date. They'd met at a Southern Christian Leadership Conference meeting in the summer of 1963. Nan was driven and had her sights set on success, in spite of the odds stacked against her. At twenty-two, she had launched a successful tailoring enterprise with her sister that paid their way through Spelman. Daniel was eighteen, barely emerging from his life of insulated privilege and about to begin his freshman year as a philosophy major at Emory University. When he first asked her out, she involuntarily laughed in his face. Life had demanded she be practical. He had the luxury of giving himself over to romance.

After four rejections, a half-dozen marigold bouquets and countless poorly performed Spanish guitar songs, Daniel's persistence paid off. Though Nan insisted she'd only agreed to the date because she was embarrassed for him, in truth, she was scared. Given that sharing the same straw as a white man was enough to incite racial violence, she was sure that neither of their communities—let alone the dominant white culture—would ever accept their relationship.

But after that first date at the Varsity, Nan knew she was in trouble. Daniel's determined infatuation had awakened the poetry in her heart—a muse that would come to define the very essence of who she was. For five years they met in secret, using their activist meetings as a cover for their rendezvous. During those tumultuous years—when an end to the violent subjugation of civil liberties seemed far from sight—they clung to each other for support like lone warriors against an unjust world.

Only Nan's sister, Sarah Ann, knew of the affair. She was Nan's maid-of-honor at the wedding. Nan recalled that warm, breezy September day as she stared at the edge of Sarah Ann's marigold bouquet forever captured in the left-hand corner of the faded, matte photograph that now stood on Daniel's desk. Nan turned her attention on the young couple in the portrait. Young Daniel's effulgent smile contrasted starkly with the anguished frown fixed upon her present husband's face as he lifted the scotch to his lips and slugged it down in one quick gulp.

Nan moved to comfort her husband, but his body involuntarily jerked in retreat as she advanced.

"I'm sorry," he said, her hurt look momentarily penetrating his own sorrow. "I just—I need some space right now."

"Okay. Okay, I get that," she replied, concerned yet understanding.

"Do you ever feel like it's all just a cruel game?" asked Daniel. He spoke with the loss of one who had already seen the petty, creeping pace of tomorrow.

"What?"

"This life."

"What are you talking about, Daniel? What happened?" questioned Nan, her tone more direct. Nan was used to Daniel's maudlin musings, and though she could usually sit with his emotional process, her tiredness that day offered her no patience for his sentimentality. A sheen of sweat formed on her face as the fireplace blasted its heat in her direction.

He looked at her, studying the fierce steadiness of her gaze, unsure of his next move. When he could no longer decipher his own emotional quagmire to meet the assuredness of her question, he looked down at his empty glass and slumped deeper into his chair.

"I feel so old," he muttered.

Ever since the dizziness and pain from the atherosclerosis began, Daniel had become sullen and cold. His general anxiety gave way to extreme moodiness and fits of anger. Nan's own descents into darkness provided the empathy she needed to tolerate her husband's continued wrestlings with mortality. But the past several months had taken their toll on her reserve. This evening she didn't have the energy to deal with his fraught philosophical examinations.

"I know," she spoke, exhaustion rolling through her body as she exhaled. Nan tentatively leaned against the doorframe, uncertain whether she should remain or leave. The sudden wind blasting from the open front door froze the sweat that dripped down her back.

Daniel turned his tired eyes back on his wife and weakly muttered, "I-I don't want to pretend anymore."

An icy chill pierced Nan, penetrating the space behind her heart. She held her breath and tightly gripped the wooden frame as the growing coldness threatened to topple her.

"What don't you want to pretend?" she asked with every bit of steel she could muster.

"I'm having an affair. I *was* having an affair," he flatly replied.

Nan dug her fingers into the wood, her knuckles mottling into shades of brown, pink and blue. The pain of splintered wood digging under her nails served as a momentary distraction from the mortal blow his words had just delivered.

"Was it one of your students?" she blurted out.

"What?" he exclaimed in disbelief. "No, of course not. Someone you don't know. Outside the academic world."

"Who then?" pressed Nan.

"No one. It doesn't matter anyway. I don't even know why I'm telling you now that it's over. I guess I just needed someone to tell."

Daniel's voice choked and tears formed in the corners of his eyes. Nan could see he was trying to stifle his emotions, but his heartbreak was getting the best of him.

"How long did it last?" demanded Nan.

Daniel stared at Nan for a moment, wondering how or why her question was relevant.

"How. Long."

"About a year," he feebly replied.

Right around the time his heart began giving him trouble, thought Nan. Daniel's behavior over the past year came into sharp focus. The distance. The coldness. The moodiness. Nan had known something had shifted in him but attributed the change to fears surrounding his declining health. She had overlooked the truth that he was also carrying a lie.

"I-I don't know what to say," she stammered as blood began to flush through her once more.

"Don't say anything," he firmly requested.

"How can I not?" she questioned, her tone rising in pitch and volume. "You come waltzing in here, tell me you're having an affair and expect me to *not* say something?"

"Honey, don't split your infinitives. You know better than that. It drives me crazy."

"Goddammit!" screamed Nan, throwing a first edition copy of D.H. Lawrence's *Lady Chatterley's Lover* at Daniel's head. He ducked just before her literary missile smacked his shocked face.

"The hell, Nan?!"

"No Daniel, you don't get to do that."

"Do what?"

"Act so flippantly about this. You don't get to avoid this conversation by making a joke and pushing me away. Not this time."

"Oh, you're definitely one to talk." He caustically threw the words at her like a wounded animal protecting its life.

"What the hell do you mean by that?" she angrily demanded.

"You think I don't know? You think I don't see you over by your bookshelf all damned day and night?"

Blood drained from Nan's face as his words sank into her.

"What do you mean by that?" she tentatively asked.

"I know about Isabelle."

It was Nan's turn to fight back tears as she recalled the yearlong love affair she'd had thirty years prior—one that ended tragically when Isabelle's unexpected seizure led to a fatal head injury. Nan closed her eyes and clutched her chest as if trying to stuff the open secret back into her locked heart. Daniel relentlessly continued to speak.

"You think I haven't watched you for years wandering around your books day and night?" he asked, more hurt than angry. Nan stared at him dumbfounded—a lifetime of pain knocking the wind out of her. Shaking with rage and despair, she curled her hands into fists, unsure whether to run away or attack him.

"You read my letters?" she finally choked out.

He guiltily said nothing, his own complicity in their mutual lie having been revealed.

Nan continued, "You went through my things? Invaded my privacy? You made assumptions about things you can't even begin to understand."

"How could I understand?! You never gave me the option. I begged you to tell me what was going on with you. Why you felt like you needed to end your life. But any time I broached the subject all I got was a wall of silence. What the hell else did you expect me to do? The only way I could connect with you was through the letters of some woman you were fucking."

He leapt from his chair and knocked over the crystal rocks glass, a gift from his parents on their wedding day. It fell to the ground—shattering the vessel into a thousand tiny shards. The wind tore through the house once more, banging the front door against the foyer wall. Without thinking, Nan stormed over to the entryway and used the weight of her entire body to forcefully slam the door shut. She kept her tight fists pinned to the cherry wood and dropped her forehead against the brass knocker.

"I never fucked her," Nan said after a few moments of catching her breath.

"What?" Daniel asked, as the door had muffled Nan's voice.

"I. Never. Fucked. Her," replied Nan, ferocity building inside her. She whipped around to face her husband as confusion clouded his tired face.

"Not in the coarse way that you mean," clarified Nan. "But, oh, how she fucked me—with her words. With her insights. With her passion. With her understanding. And yes, with her perfect hands that knew every inch of my hungry body."

Daniel continued to watch Nan as she spoke, his confusion morphing into a cocktail of grief and fury.

"Do you know what it's like to have found someone so like you that when you're with them you just merge into one being? One body? One soul?"

Nan began shaking her head as tears poured down her soft cheeks.

"That's what it was like to be with her. For years after Ella was born, I felt you pull away from me. I knew I loved you, but I felt you leaving our marriage."

Daniel inhaled sharply and answered back, "You left the marriage the moment Sarah Ann died."

Nan collapsed into the door as his words, like arrows, ripped through her chest. Spurred on by his own growing anger, Daniel stomped over to the bookshelf and pulled out a thin collection of poems, the spine worn from years of use. Inside the book were pages of purple stationary neatly folded between the book's leaves as well as three pressed marigolds—long dead yet delicately preserved. He marched over to Nan and forcefully presented the book and its clandestine contents to her.

"Here. Take it. Take your dead sister's poetry and your lover's old letters and these—dead flowers. How apropos."

Daniel callously flipped through the yellowed pages while Nan stared aghast at his relentless brutality.

"Take them. You've chosen them over me. Here. Take them."

They remained transfixed in their marital stand-off. Daniel's cold cruelty crushed Nan's heart yet galvanized her body. She steadied her legs underneath her and stood erect, facing the stranger of a man before her.

"Take them," he repeated, brandishing the pregnant paperback before her.

Without taking her steely eyes off of him, Nan wrapped her fingers around the letter-filled book. She then slowly, but firmly, reclaimed the contents from his hands and held them above her head.

"These women," she began, her voice booming, "these sisters, these mothers, these warriors have known me more than you could *ever* know me. Do not defile their memories with your tired little tantrum. These women keep me company where you do not. These ghosts are here for me to set them free!"

Daniel reflected on the loneliness that would possess a woman to retreat into the pages of the dead. It was a loneliness he, too, had come to know over the years as their hard-earned love dissipated into complacency. He recalled the numerous missed dinners because of meetings at work or out-of-town conferences. He remembering staying up late grading papers while Nan slept alone in their bed. He solemnly recollected their Sunday tradition of coffee and bagels during Ella's early years, which fell to the side as the rigors of parenting took priority. Remembering their once close intimacy, Daniel sighed as regret settled into his body. He looked at his wife with deep care and compassion.

"Nan," he softly spoke, "ghosts aren't here for freedom. They're here for haunting. If they were free, they wouldn't be ghosts."

Nan panted, taking in his words, but unwilling to budge.

"Look, Nan. I'm sorry. I didn't mean to be cruel. I just wish I knew how to help you. That's why I never said anything all these years. I was afraid of losing you to the darkness again."

Nan took in the sincerity of his words and felt the love that had always been there—just behind his pain and fear. She slowly lowered her arm and pressed the letter-filled book against her chest. A deep wail emanated from the endless void of grief as tears cascaded down her face. Daniel leaned in to comfort her, but she stepped back, unable to receive him.

"What can I do, Nan?" he asked pleadingly.

"Nothing, nothing," she replied through broken sobs. "You—you just can't understand."

"Help me!" he cried. "Help me to understand. What don't I get?"

Nan stared at him with her tear-streaked eyes as a deeper understanding unfolded within her. She inhaled and straightened her spine, rising to her full 5'3" height. Daniel noticed the shift in her stature and lowered his hands, stepping back to take in the fullness of his wife. Their breath slowed and steadied, syncing into a rhythmic cycle. They looked into each other's eyes as if finally seeing each other for the first time in years.

After a few minutes, Nan shifted her gaze and glided towards the living room chair, sitting down with the elegance of a queen. She gingerly placed the book and letters on the mahogany side table before slowly shifting her soft eyes back on to her husband.

"Do you remember when Ella first came to us and told us her name?" she asked.

Of course Daniel recalled the moment over twenty years ago. Ella had just completed nursing school in San Francisco.

She had called them, needing desperately to talk but clearly scared to speak. After a few minutes of playing cursory catch-up, Ella finally told them she was tired of lying—she no longer wanted to perform as a boy. She told them that she'd never been a boy and was ready to claim her life as a woman.

"Who we are—it all starts with a name," continued Nan.

Daniel looked at her confused but continued to follow her.

"Do you know my name, Daniel?" Nan pointedly asked.

"What are you talking about?" he replied, his confusion growing.

Nan looked at Daniel for a moment before stating, "My name isn't Nan. It's Nnenne. Nan was more socially acceptable."

Daniel stared at her flabbergasted.

"Nnenne," he repeated, the wind knocked out of him.

"Yes. It means 'mother's mother.' Sarah Ann was Nnenna. 'Father's mother.' These names are often given when it is believed the child is the reincarnation of her maternal or paternal grandmother. Our parents named us this so we would always remember where we came from."

Daniel furrowed his brows as he searched her eyes for some sort of clarity. He finally gave up trying to understand and simply walked over to the chair facing Nan, collapsing into its leathery folds in a fleshy heap.

"Why didn't you think to tell me this?" he asked after several seconds of silence.

"You never thought to ask," she answered. "But she did."

Nan gestured towards her dead lover's faded letters stuffed between her dead twin's faded poetry. Her small hand rested on the pile of papers as Daniel watched, enraptured by the woman unfolding before him. Nan thumbed her way through the papers and gently procured one folded purple sheet from the entangled stack. As Nan scanned the page's perfectly curled cursive handwriting, her stoic resolve began to crumble into profound longing. Nan closed her eyes as the memories danced before her.

"Even though Isabelle was the same age as I, she came to me like a child. Eager. Infatuated. Yearning for guidance. Her innocence was my undoing. She hung on my every word as if it were buried treasure. I'd never had every part of me so thoroughly enjoyed: mind, body, heart, soul."

A tear landed on the page, smearing the blue ink. Nan felt the drop hit the paper and opened her eyes. She took the edge of her red, angora sweater and blotted the moisture—attempting to preserve the perfect lettering.

When she had completed the delicate task, she turned her eyes upon her husband and said, "It was the most erotic experience of my life. And ultimately, it's what saved me from, as you say, being lost to the darkness."

Daniel exhaled, grateful to finally receive what he'd been missing all these years—her vulnerability and her truth. He felt small before the great woman before him, yet he also yearned to be near her. Daniel's corporeal heap slunk to the ground, and—like a baby—he crawled his way over to his wife. When he placed his head in her lap, the folds of her long, black skirt circled his face like a swaddled infant. She smoothed his thinning hair with her tired hands.

"Yes, sweet one," she whispered. "We can let go now."

Her permission unbolted the final hindrance to his pain. He clutched the black fabric of her skirt in his fists as an abyss yawned across his chest—despair and remorse spilling forth. He sobbed the sobs of a young child: pure, uninhibited and undiluted with shame.

"I'm sorry," he repeatedly lamented. "I'm sorry. I'm sorry. I'm sorry."

Nan continued to stroke his head even as his tears soaked her dress. He held on to her as if he were returning home. His rounded shoulders jumped with each desperate gasp of air he took between sobs. Nan's own grief melted into rivers of compassion for this man—someone she knew long ago but had somehow lost over time. They had been through so much together in their early years: Kennedy, Malcolm, King, Kennedy again. But when the social causes that bound them shifted with the tides of history, the communal fight they had shared slowly slipped into complacent domesticity—not realizing until decades later they were each looking into the eyes of a stranger.

"Tell me about her," inquired Nan once Daniel's weeping had started to abate.

"Who?" he asked.

"Your other woman. You know about mine. Tell me: what did you love about her?"

Daniel looked at her with momentary disbelief before shrugging his shoulders and answering.

"She made me feel young again. Like anything was possible. Like who I was could make a difference." He paused and took Nan's hand in his before saying, "To be honest, she made me feel like you used to back when we first met."

Nan smiled as she squeezed his hand.

"Do you want that again?" she asked.

"Yes!" he emphatically exclaimed. "More than anything."

"Then choose it," she said.

He stared at her unsure of the challenge she was setting.

Nan clarified, "If you want me, you have to choose me."

Nan released his hand from hers and lifted her body off the chair, looking down at her husband's crumpled heap on the crimson Moroccan rug.

"Stand up and *choose* your wife."

Daniel pushed himself up onto his knees and beheld the stunning woman before him.

"I-I'm not sure I know how," he stammered.

"You will remember," she pointedly remarked.

Her confidence solidified his resolve. Daniel clasped the edge of the chair and hoisted himself to standing. He looked his wife in the eyes, breathing in her strength and ferocity. He then took her hand and, without saying a word, led her up the staircase to their bedroom. The white and blue quilt Nan had made as an anniversary present hung over the edge of the cherry sleigh bed. Daniel smoothed out the duvet covers and guided Nan to lie down onto its softness.

He paused, unsure what to do next. Sensing his hesitancy, Nan smiled.

"Not unlike the first time," she said with a smirk on her face.

Daniel laughed remembering how confident he had pretended to be when he wooed her but how utterly frightened he was the moment she undressed.

"I promise not to throw up this time," he replied.

She giggled at the memory of Daniel, naked, with his head in the toilet.

"That wasn't so bad. Made for a good story. And anyway, you were a fast learner."

Her words emboldened Daniel. He placed his hands on her ankles just below the hem of her skirt and slid his palms over her shins and thighs, exposing her thin legs. He lightly ran his fingers on the inside of her thigh, admiring its softness. She sighed and opened her legs wider. He smiled when he noticed the pink lace panties Nan wore—recognizing the sensual young woman he fell in love with decades ago. He gently pinched the edges of her undergarments and slid them off. Nan giggled coyly, like a teenager exposing herself to a lover for the first time. She eagerly pulled her sweater over her head, revealing a matching pink bra underneath. She reached around to her back, unhooked the bra's clasp and lowered the straps from her sloped shoulders, swiftly removing it. She then untied her wrap skirt's sash and unraveled it from her waist. Her body, unencumbered by her clothing, yawned open towards Daniel as he stood by the bed, watching her.

When she had settled, he climbed onto the bed next to her, sitting by her side and bringing her right leg across his lap. He placed one hand on her chest and looked into her eyes. They held still in the pregnant space—their unified breath the only movement. He then softly cupped her pussy with his free hand, gently pressing up towards her head. Nan hiked her left knee higher, exposing herself even more. He reduced his pressure between her thighs and lightly caressed her coarse hairs with the back of his fingers.

He stopped and told Nan to turn onto her belly. She obeyed. He put his fingers into her shoulder blades and tenderly squeezed, giving permission to her muscles—held rigid by unexpressed joy, anger and grief—to let go. Her body melted under his touch.

He then slowly guided her to her right side—her chest facing him. He lifted her left leg over his shoulder and pulled her right tightly against him. He wrapped his arms around her back, binding her torso to his. Nan relished the feeling of being restrained while simultaneously spreading herself wide open. Feeling her eager responsiveness, Daniel freed one of his hands and slowly slid his fingers inside her. He delicately stroked the inside of her slick walls, simultaneously relaxing and priming her. His thumb occasionally grazed the hot electricity of her clit. She pressed her hips against his hands, yearning for more. His body braced her with each stroke—containing her unfolding warmth.

Then he shifted her onto her back. His fingers deep inside of her, he drew her forth—tapping sap from an ancient, fertile tree. Her pussy contracted rhythmically with her heartbeat. He stroked up. A rush of heat rolled over her left foot and calf—almost too hot to bear. She felt like crying—so she breathed and surrendered another layer. Nan wanted to feel all of this.

As the burning dissipated through her feet, Nan floated back down into a gray, clear pool, hovering just above the water's edge. Inside her, his fingers pressed upward, while his other hand continued to stroke her clit.

She relaxed deeper and chanted, "There is nothing to fear."

Upon her words, two women materialized from behind Daniel. One held a bouquet of fresh marigolds. The other clutched a stack of purple letters. Nan welcomed their presence as each woman took one of her hands.

Nan sunk deeper into her body, feeling something hidden wanting to emerge. A round, bulbous heat—a burning pleasure—snowballed as it moved from her heart to her belly to her clit. She kept relaxing as the heat opened to a canyon of potential—its waxing intensity causing her to contract a little.

"What if you just say yes?" Nan thought to herself.

"Yes," she whispered, relaxing into the misty ocean of sensation pulling her further out to sea.

Nan felt the fog-tide rolling over her feet, inching over her surrender. The cool fog-water made its way up her ankles, thighs, pussy, belly, arms, chest, head. Her whole body bathed in this force. There was no thrashing around in the midst of this orgasm—only a stilled hush. She exhaled as more of the sparkly, fog-water rolled over—suspending her in what felt like eternity.

And then, as softly as it came in, it rolled away. Despite the spectral presence of her dead lover and sister, the connection between all of them was undeniably human and expanded beyond anything she could remember. She had forgotten time. It was in this moment Nan realized how very lonely she had been. Not just in this life but for lifetimes. Nan began shaking and weeping.

"Oh God," she cried out, "I miss God."

Unbearable love pressed against her chest. It was a spherical expansion that cracked the edges of her ribs and tore through her skin. As her heart burst forward, the back of her body burned—like simultaneously giving birth to wings and dying in the phoenix's flames. An involuntary wave of gratitude and grief gripped her throat, and she keened an ancient sound that twisted with both agony and wonder.

"We touched love," she thought. "Not ephemeral romance, that crunches and pounces and cramps. But love. Pure. Rich. Golden. Love."

She cried. And cried. And cried. Isabelle skimmed Nan's hand against her lips, delivering soft kisses to Nan's trembling fingers. Sarah Ann placed her sister's hand against her own ghostly, unbeating heart. Daniel released his hold on Nan and pressed his palms solidly against her pubic bone, grounding her.

As Nan began to drop back to earth, she murmured with a hint of embarrassment, "I miss God."

More tears flowed and a bubble rose in her throat as she realized what really needed to be said. The embers of resentment, anger, loss and loneliness had settled on top of the words and threatened to keep her silent, but the desire to speak was so powerful that to hold back would feel like a slow, burning death.

"I love you. I love you so much."

The women looked at Nan with care and sweetness. Daniel smiled with awe and reverence for his newborn wife. Nan noticed the shirt Daniel wore was the exact color as the one they got married in. She giggled as she recalled his ridiculous peach frills.

"I like that color on you," she finally gasped, speaking her thoughts before they slipped away. All four of them laughed.

The ephemeral peak inevitably passed as they all held one another—deeply immersed in a raw warmth humming between their bodies. Present. Nothing else to do but feel. Just Nan—and the ones who taught her how to love.

After some time, the two ghosts finally stepped back, releasing Nan to the living world. She realized then that the ghosts weren't there for their own freedom. They came to guide Nan to her liberation. She watched as they dissolved back into the fog—a place Nan knew she would call home when her time came.

Daniel lifted the edges of the comforter around Nan's temporary corpse. He unfolded the anniversary quilt from the edge of the bed and placed it like a shroud over her face and body. He lay beside her as they both floated to sleep.

• • •

Daniel's slumbered shifting woke Nan from her liminal dream state. She softly unwound herself from her husband's limbs and tiptoed down the creaking staircase. The grandfather clock struck midnight as she cast her eyes upon the table where the book and letters lay. Deliberately, she walked past them towards the craft dresser full of cards, wrapping paper and packaging materials. She rummaged around the drawers until she found a large swath of blood-colored velvet and a long ribbon of raffia.

She returned to the small table and sat in the chair next to it. She laid the velvet across her naked thighs and placed the book and letters on top of the fabric's warm softness. She gently peeled each marigold from the book's warped pages—where they'd made their home since Sarah Ann's funeral. She returned the book and letters to the table and, like swaddling a sleeping child, she delicately folded the felted corners over the stiff orange petals. When the bundle was wrapped to her satisfaction, she carefully tied the raffia around it.

Nan made her way to the house's back entrance. She stepped onto the patio, the cool moonlight reflecting off her bare skin. Her feet silently padded down the wooden steps and made their way through the chilly grass to the crabapple tree at the edge of the fenced backyard. She dropped to her knees and clawed her way through a patch of dirt with bare hands. When she'd made a hole big enough for the parcel, she dropped it into the crater's concave center and methodically piled handfuls of soil on the sanguine offering. Once it was covered, she unceremoniously packed the top layer of the grave, stood up and stepped back in to the warm, dimly lit house. Returning home.

PART THREE

invitation

> *Love is an attempt to penetrate another being,*
> *but it can only be realized if the surrender is mutual.*
> *~ Octavio Paz, trans. Lysander Kemp,*
> The Labyrinth of Solitude and Other Writings

the morning after

Cool raindrops dot the window
As our melted warmth insulates us from
The liquid Sunday morning
(Gray skies forming
A cozy backdrop
For our scene).

My bare thigh resting
On your pajama-ed leg.
My right hand slipped
Under your left,
As my palm inhales
The heat from your ribs.

You hover on the edge
Of a waking snooze.
A soft snore rises
From your throat.
A moment frozen
With desire…

This
    could
  go
       in
     any
direction.

CANDICE DAWN

On the one hand,
I'd hate to disturb your sweet surrender,
Captured like a nostalgic portrait
Studied by professors
And glanced over by disinterested tourists
As they rush through the gallery.

On the other hand,
I want nothing more
Than to feel
Your lips brushing the side of my neck;
Your tongue tracing the curve of my breasts;
Your fingers twisting inside of me.

Another soft snore.
A resigned sigh.
I pull my hand out from your shirt
In one cottony stroke.
Unraveling from you,
I tiptoe towards the door,

Turning in time
To see your lazy smile
And half-opened eyes.
"I'll let you get some rest," I whisper,
As the door firmly latches
Behind my back.

epilogue

Now like Persephone, we stand here emerging from the underworld, with the fertile seeds of our hibernation ready to burst forth. Naked, we behold the ashen phoenix-mirror, once ablaze in the cleansing fire of truth, staring at the maiden form before us. Touching our still-raw skin, perhaps we find ourselves lost in the unrecognizable folds of our freshly forged bodies. Perhaps an old soul, glimmering from the past, stares at us through wise eyes—the one who always knew our greatness during our years of doubt. Who we are after a voyage is never who we were before. The new landscapes shift our vision of what's possible—"home" transforms into an old lover with whom we've reunited, both familiar and virgin.

Here is where the real work of the heroine's journey begins. With the burning lessons from our soul-trek still smoldering in our hearts, we must now integrate them into our daily lives. We must rediscover the erotic, over and over again, within the gorgeous and mystical miracle of mundanity. We must cultivate the *discipline* to unwaveringly walk the path of eros. But remember, discipline is not denial. There is no extra merit to be gained from living as a spiritual martyr. In fact, denial only stunts our spiritual maturity, for the fruits of eros include ecstatic service to the divine and inspiring others with our joy—both of which nourish the hungriest parts of ourselves.

Discipline is simply presence and commitment to knowing the true capacity of our soul-shaking, soul-quaking, soul-waking love. Since we are trained to be terrified of receiving this, we often settle for addictive, pseudo-erotic hits, decreasing our capacity to feel. But as Audre Lorde clarifies, "The erotic is not a question only of what we do; it is a question of how acutely and fully we can feel in the doing."[33] We honor it all—the pain, the pleasure, the light, and the dark—by staying awake and knowing when to emerge from the chrysalis of transformation.

My hope is that this book has inspired you to take the first steps on your own journey of erotic awakening. The world needs our mature, unified, erotic chorus guiding us back to the reconnection and rehumanization of culture. The page before this one is blank. That blank page is an invitation, the surface upon which to write your unique erotic story. An erotic life is a holy life, where pleasure is our power and desire is our prayer.

So remember: though we have reached the end of this chapter, the heroine's journey has only just begun. Welcome home.

---

[33] Lorde, 53.